S0-CPT-940

Cup of Cold Water

OTHER BOOKS BY PAUL HUTCHENS

For Young People and Adults

THIS WAY OUT
THE VISION
SHAFTED SUNLIGHT
BLAZE STAR
MASTERING MARCUS
THE LAST FIRST
WINDBLOWN
THIS IS LIFE
A SONG FOREVER
THE VOICE
YESTERDAY'S RAIN
CUP OF COLD WATER
ECLIPSE
MORNING FLIGHT

For Boys and Girls (8-14)

THE SUGAR CREEK GANG
WE KILLED A BEAR
FURTHER ADVENTURES OF THE SUGAR CREEK GANG
THE SUGAR CREEK GANG GOES CAMPING
THE SUGAR CREEK GANG IN CHICAGO
THE SUGAR CREEK GANG IN SCHOOL
MYSTERY AT SUGAR CREEK
THE SUGAR CREEK GANG FLIES TO CUBA
ONE STORMY DAY AT SUGAR CREEK
A NEW SUGAR CREEK MYSTERY
SHENANIGANS AT SUGAR CREEK

Cup of Cold Water

by
PAUL HUTCHENS

WM. B. EERDMANS PUBLISHING COMPANY
Grand Rapids   Michigan

CUP OF COLD WATER
By Paul Hutchens

Copyright, 1941, *by*
Wm. B. Eerdmans Publishing Co.

**All rights reserved. No portion may be
reproduced without permission from the
publisher, except for brief quotations to be
used in a newspaper or magazine review.**

Eleventh Printing, May, 1958

PHOTOLITHOPRINTED BY CUSHING - MALLOY, INC.
ANN ARBOR, MICHIGAN, UNITED STATES OF AMERICA

Cup of Cold Water

1.

THE little outboard motor came to life with a roar at the first sharp pull of the starter cord. The lady pilot moved the speed control lever slightly to the right of center, pushed the mixture lever slowly in the same direction until the motor was running smoothly. Then she turned her face to the sunrise, swung the boat sharply about, opened the throttle wide and set out across the lake, which, on this windless, cloudless morning, lay before her like a great blue mirror stretching away and away to the forest of oak and pine on the other side — oak and pine and balm of Gilead and blue spruce and birch, and a countless variety of other trees.

There, on that other shore, was a wide sandy beach, along which, some twenty feet from the water's edge, marched a row of new birch, all the way down to the end of the point which pushed far out into the lake. Beyond that point was lake and more lake.

In the opposite direction, the shoreline was more rugged, and was climaxed a quarter mile farther on by a high promontory, at the base of which were jagged rocks both under and above the water.

In the water world along the edge of the beach and especially in the deeper water beyond the rocks, there lived and struggled for existence, a plethora of fish of many varieties— and with character traits so like the world of men and women which the lady pilot knew so well, and from which for a little season she had run away, — and *to* which, fatefully, she must go back again as soon as her respite was past — *unless* — her venture were successful.

To-day, however, was hers, — to-day and tomorrow and all this month. After that . . . She would not think of *after that!*

In that underwater world, she was thinking now, as her boat grooved its way toward the sandy beach on the other

side, were wary, acrobatic bass, gorging themselves with too
much food, like the pig-faced man who sometimes ate directly
across from her in the cafe in the city she had left behind;
there were voracious, spatulate-snouted great northern which
hid themselves in the weeds, waiting for the flash of a fin of a
lesser fish, when with the speed of a torpedo and with the
same mercilessness, they would shoot through the water in
one swift furious rush. There would be the blind seizure of
the victim, the tearing of flesh, the swallowing — and victim-
ized life would give itself to sustain other life. . .

There were men in the business world like that. Bailes
Martini, her employer, was like that. She was glad to be free
from him for a season. She could not understand the willing-
ness with which he had let her go.

And Jim Grabill was like the walleye pike, not in appear-
ance — for he was strikingly handsome, — but in his manner of
pursuit: following along behind, nibbling at the bait, always
nibbling, always pursuing — first one bait and then another.
Yet he had never been caught, — except for a little while, and
then, for some reason had been thrown back as undesirable . . .

Jim! The lady pilot too, had thrown him back, and for
reasons.

Straight ahead, the boat parting the water like a plow, leaving behind a widening trail of churning wavelets . . . It was
good to be alive, so very much alive, so alert to things, so free
in spite of being bound by responsibilities, free especially
from slavery to Martini: the rush of money-making traffic, the
professional smiles and frowns and "thank you's" and "I'm
sorry, but Mr. Martini is not in," "He is busy now," — "No, he
is in consultation." Click-click-clickety-click-click-click . . .
Typewriter keys spelling out fifty words a minute; roller-bear-
ing files opening and closing, telephone calls to make or cancel
or answer . . . "Yes, Mr. Martini, the forms are ready . . ."

In that cyclonic world there were things to *do* only; here,
there were things to *love*: the never-the-same lake — blue or
gray or tinted as the sky's mood might dictate. Always the colors of the sky and the lake were the same; their moods also; for
these two, the sky and the lake, had been wedded long ago by

the Maker of them both; yet the one took its color and its mood from the other — the lake from the sky, — and never was the order reversed.

Back in that other world, Jim would receive, this morning probably, delivered to his apartment by special messenger, the final answer to his many proposals. In expensive robe and slippers, he would traverse the soft Kavara rug on the hall floor, to answer the bell. In the long mirror in the hall, he would smile, perhaps, at the brown-haired, azure-eyed reflection of himself, see the firm set of broad shoulders slightly stooped, pause a moment to push back with soft, daintily groomed hands, a misplaced lock of hair.

Holding the special delivery letter in his hand, postmarked by a railway mail clerk — she had mailed it on the train so he would not know where to find her — he would open it and read:

"My Dear Jim:

"Now that we understand each other, I am sure you will try to forget how deeply you have been hurt. I have never coveted your world at all — anyway, not its philosophies nor its behaviour, only perhaps its luxury, and that because of its freedom from routine, so that I could have time to do the one thing above all others that I know I must do. I could never have entered with you into the life you have offered. Such luxury and life would be very boring and empty.

"I cannot be satisfied merely to *have*. I must *do*. And I must *be!*

"Consider this letter a final good-bye, Jim; go on back to your pleasures if you must, which, you know, are only for a season. I have gone away for a long time, to rest as well as to work. Some day, when you will have read my book, you will understand better the motives that are urging me on. If I fail, which I dare not, I can still go back to Martini from whose slavery you have offered to free me, but I most certainly do not wish to be a new satellite in the social sky.

"Yours sincerely,

"BERYL LANE."

The pilot of the little rowboat shooting out across the lake, looked down at the trim blue and white oxfords that sheathed her equally trim feet. She was wearing an all new outfit this morning. In imagination, looking over Jim Grabill's shoulder as he read her letter, trying to read his mind also, she saw herself as she was at this moment; her autumn-leaf hair tucked into a blue snood, herself looking very slender in what the fashion world called "rayon sharkskin" — a snow white dress, blue-belted and buttoned all the way down in front. The Maker of the sky and the lake and the varicolored forest, changed *their* colors often; so also did Beryl change the color and style of her clothes, not to be garish but to be neat and attractive, not to make unwary fish go blind with infatuation or admiration, but to satisfy her own appreciation of things beautiful. Clothes could be beautiful and still be modest, she thought.

The letter, she knew now more certainly than ever, was the very truth. It would have been selling her soul, to have married Jim. It would have been chaining herself to earth, when what she desired more than anything else was to soar and soar, high above sordid things, to where she could not hear the din of noisy pleasures, nor drink the bitter cup which indulgence demanded — *afterward!*

The pleasures of sin for a season! Moses of old, had chosen to suffer afflictions with the people of God, rather than to enjoy them. . . . And now, with the wind in her face, the smell of the lake in her nostrils, the roar of the little motor in her ears, the laughter of the water as it gave way gladly to her boat, the dip and toss and tumble of the white gulls playing in the sky world, the thrill of freedom because of her isolation from the money-making noise of the city, and from Jim's ceaseless pursuit — *now* she was beginning to thrill to the new life which lay before her like an uncharted lake, yet which had been charted by One Who knew all the future, and Who, when he putteth forth His own sheep, goeth before them . . .

For a moment she turned, looked back at the receding shore-line whence she had come, with its little row of alike cottages, each with its green roof and screened porch, each with a stone chimney; and on the inside of each, a wide fireplace, comfortable chairs, a bedroom, kitchenette and table. On the table in her own cottage were her portable typewriter, reference books, ink and writing tablets. Carefully stored away in a cabinet file beside the table was her growing manuscript, which, some day, would build itself into a book. Already it was well along toward completion. . . . This was why she could not enter Jim's world, — Jim's pleasure world, for she must write and write and write. People in Jim's world were living artificially, their pleasures were tinselled with lies. They were bubble pleasures that burst always at the moment of their highest beauty, because their beauty was, perhaps, only an illusion. . . .

The elm tree standing in front of her cottage was like a gaunt old giant this morning, it's first great limb stretched out like a mighty arm, like the arm of a similar tree on the farm of her old home. There had been a swing on the old maple — Sugar Tree, the children had called it.

She turned her eyes back to the lake, watched the sun pushing its way through pink curtains to give the day more light, and knew that for her a new day was dawning. The manuscript now nearing its final chapters, would grow until it was complete, and some day she would read her name in gold below the title. "Fan" letters from enthusiastic readers would find their place in bulging files to be remembered in the years that would find her with graying hair. Checks signed with her own name would arrive weekly, or monthly in the tin mail box in the old home five hundred miles away. A gray, round little mother, sighing over summer canning and winter anxiety because of the pinch of poverty, would open the letters from her successful daughter, cash those checks at the Brown Market and ride home in the family's battered car, her market basket laden — and there would be contentment in the home, contentment and the sense of well-being that accompanied social security.

It was a daring thing she was undertaking, — but she believed she was following some kind of leading. She could not be sure, but she must believe she was right. She might never marry at all, not if her book were a success, and its popularity demanded another, and another. She would not have time then to give to a husband or to children, or to the routine of home-making. . . .

It was the sermon she had heard that dreary morning three months ago that had been the first link in the chain. . . .

There were many links now; and today, and tomorrow and during the next week, she would forge another. Strange title for a sermon, she thought —*had* thought that day; but when she had come to understand its meaning, it had already intertwined itself in her philosophy of life, and had already brought its results. The sermon title would be the title also of the book she must write. . . .

It was all so strange, so like an adventure, — this following of the thoughts and whims of her characters, suffering them to do as they wished, *feeling* their problems, their heartaches, making them do her bidding, yet allowing them freedom of will; predestining them to certain acts and thoughts, yet letting them think and act of themselves. This, she told herself, was a work of art, of creation even — *sub*-creation, under the supervision and enduement of the Creator Himself.

Writing, she had discovered, was not only interesting and adventurous; it was also strenuous. It required the giving of one's self to the discipline and monotony of staying on the job, even when the lake called and teased her to come and splash in its waters, or go gliding over its surface in the little rowboat that was beached at the dock. . . .

Writing was more, too, than painting in word colors the beautiful philosophy of that morning's sermon. Philosophy, to come alive, must be clothed—rather, it must clothe—*living* human beings. It could live only in life itself. . . .

And so, this radiant morning, she had set out in search of life. On that other shore, nestled among the oak and basswood, behind the breastworks of new birch, she had seen with

her binoculars, and also from close range, when motor-boating, a snow-white house, set like a white castle among the
green. An old man lived there, she knew. She had seen him
there, moving among the flowers; and every day, in his little
dinghy, with its outboard motor put-putting, he would en-
circle the lake, his fishing rod at his side, trolling for the temperamental walleye pike. Once he had beached his dinghy
beside her own white rowboat at her dock, and with the aid
of his silver-topped cane, had hobbled up the board walk to
her cabin, carrying a string of walleye. . . .

"Good morning," he had wheezed in a raspy, worn-out
voice. He had displayed, waist-high, his morning's catch. "Re-
frigerator is full of them, and I need a change of diet. Can
you use two or three, maybe . . . ?"

He stopped in the middle of his question, and adjusted his
weather-blurred, double-lense glasses. "I used to have a daughter who was a nurse." She had been wearing her white outfit
that morning.

He swallowed his Adam's apple, and busied himself with
his string of fish. "I'll leave you two," he said, and a little
later was on his way. She watched him go, his silver-topped
cane in one hand, his string of fish in the other. He struggled
along in the little footpath that wound among the basswood
and Indian cherry — with here and there a bit of poison ivy.
He made the round of the dozen or more cottages along the
shore, and when he came back a little later, his stringer was
empty. Here, she decided, was a character who would be colorful in the pages of her book. She followed him out to the
dock and watched him getting ready to shove off. He apolo-
gized for his shortness of breath, saying, "Heart's not so good
any more. Getting near the time when it'll have to take a
long rest."

Still short of breath, he sat down on the edge of the dock.
He was a very lovable old gentleman, she thought, and before she knew it she was telling of her book, and more particularly of its theme. Afterward she wondered why she had
opened her heart to him in so much confidence, why she had

told him of the cloud of debt that hung so heavily over the old home and how, if she could only give all her time to writing, —

He had interrupted at that point, asking, "How much is the mortgage?" And she had told him.

"I have a nephew who is writing a book," he said. "He's a college professor." The words pictured in her mind a be-whiskered, sedate, middle-aged professor, barricaded behind spectacles and a mahogany desk.

"This your first book?" he wanted to know.

"My very first," she replied. "By profession I'm a stenographer in a law office. I write out insurance policies, make wills and do things like that, things I ought not to be doing, because I know I can write stories that will win souls —"

He frowned. "Wills, did you say?" He coughed, and immediately his mind seemed to be astray on things of interest to himself. He shuffled off the dock, climbed into his dinghy. She helped him get started.

"Drive over and see my flowers some time," he said, while he coiled the starter cord around the starting disc.

"I will," she promised.

There was a roar of motor, and the old man was off, leaving behind him an atmosphere that was redolent with the philosophy of the sermon of that Sunday morning. The next day he had come again and had talked with her about her new book. She had read him portions of it to his delight, and in his quaint way he had offered suggestions which she discovered were excellent. On that day, watching him as he motored back across the lake, she had, by the peculiar legerdemain known to fiction writers, converted him into a young man, handsome and worthy to be the hero of her story, to play opposite the lovely heroine.

And while she watched, she had been vacuumed into the strange play world of her book. Her thoughts flew hither and yon in an abandon that was no less free than the wind which at that moment was blowing her hair about her face . . . The man in the boat became her lover, driving away for only a little while, then he would come back to her; a young man with ideals and faith in Christ . . .

It had been a new experience, and thrilling to think of her hero in this way — his white boat plowing through the waves, above him the white gulls circling, dipping, tumbling in careless rhythm. The white house yonder became a turreted castle in which her hero lived, and for a moment — only a moment — she too lived there, and was the princess who moved with him among his flowers . . . She rode the waves with him, walked beside him through the winding forest trails; and on a cool evening, she sat in a great chair before the fireplace which she knew must be there . . . A servant, perhaps, would come and go with trays, and he, the man of her book, would sit beside her. Together, they would live out the beautiful philosophy of the sermon she had heard that morning in the city three months ago, apply its principles to all their world, and especially to their own relationships — and there would be in their home, whatever or wherever it might be, no rough and cruel friction such as had at times characterized her own home three hundred miles away — the smoke of which friction had hung always like a shadow over the family. That smoke had been like the smoke of war clouds, and had blinded their eyes to the finer things of life . . . and love. There had been so little love.

Mother was happy now, however, not because Father was dead, but because she was living for the first time in many years — and if the cloud of poverty could be removed too . . .

The cloud of poverty *would* be removed! Not because Beryl would marry Jim Grabill, but because her book would succeed . . . It would *have* to succeed! . . .

Her best writing hours, she had discovered, were in the early morning, before the general world of men was awake, and when her mind was most alert . . .

She steered now, straight for the beach beside the dock. With a quick, routine movement, she closed the gasoline shut-off valve, closed the air-vent screw, noticed that without thinking, she had made other proper adjustments. The control lever was at its extreme left position, and the propellor lifted free from the sand on the shallow lake-bottom.

The prow of her row-boat scraped against the sand of the beach beside the old man's dinghy, in which, left in neat arrangement as if in preparation for a fishing trip, were an expensive casting rod, a steel, gray-enamelled tackle-box, a landing net and a book. The book, wearing a plain two-color dust jacket, lay half-covered with a life-buoy cushion in the stern. A high-powered outboard motor clung to the stern, near which, tied to the side of the boat, was a minnow pail in which were both live and dead chubs. Live chubs, she thought, were walleye pike bait, and thought also of Jim Grabill, who had lived in her past, but who now held no attraction for her. She was dead to him and he to her. If only he had been different! . . .

She lifted the pail, changed the water. The old man had probably been fishing already this morning, and, coming back, had neglected to set the inner, screened part of the pail out into the lake. She did not like minnows to die unnecessarily.

On the shore, Beryl, only comfortably aware of her attractive outfit — blue-and-white shoes, autumn-leaf hair tucked into blue snood, the all-white dress — walked the stone path toward the stoop at the gate of the house, which, she noticed, led into an arched loggia, above the entrance of which, in polished copper letters, were spelled the words:

THE NEST.

She would ask the kind old fisherman if she might word-paint The Nest, the beautiful lawn with its many flowers, and the dock and beach with the boats.

She stopped under a rose-shaded pergola at the edge of the walk and wrote, using the shorthand system she knew so well, and which she had used so many times in Martini's inner office — so many thousands of times. Her employer now was not the grizzle-browed, spatulate-snouted Martini, but an invisible one — the voice of her ambition, dictating slowly and with carefully studied phrases, the scene before her: The two white boats at the dock with their outboard motors tilted forward, their propellers touching only the surface of the water; the winding stone path that led from the dock to the latticed gate of the loggia; the Nest itself whose main facade was visible from her own cabin far across the lake, and from which two arched eye-windows looked out . . . A sun room on the flat roof sat like a grotesque, many-eyed bird perched atop its white nest . . .

And so she wrote, dreamily, slowly, carefully. At an urn-topped bird-bath in the center of the lawn, where at that very moment a robin was performing his ablutions, she placed her heroine, pictured her with blue snood, white dress, blue-buttoned all the way down. In the unruffled water of the urn, she saw the sky, pink and gold and rose at the eastern horizon. A smile played about the lips of the girl who was mirrored there, and that girl was saying to herself the words of the text which the minister had quoted in the sermon three months ago, the central truth of which text had given life new meaning, and which, could it be enthroned in the minds of all true followers of the Man of Galilee Who had said the words, would make other minds more quickly willing to enthrone *Him* Lord of all . . . *"And whosoever shall give to drink unto one of these little ones a cup of cold water only in the name of a disciple, verily I say unto you, he shall in no wise lose his reward."*

"A cup of *COLD* water!" Anyone, in that dusty, semi-tropical climate, in which the Master lived during his earthly life, without the modern conveniences of to-day, would have discovered that it required *extra* effort to serve the cup of *cold* water. Anyone could have given warm, or luke-warm water from the reservoir in the house, but to do the *extra* thing, the thing not required, the extra-mile thing, *that* was what the Master had meant. "And *that*," the minister had declared, "will gain an entrance for you — you Christians — into many an unbelieving heart . . . When the Master would make fishers of men of rugged uncultured disciples, he gave them first, an unusually large netful of fishes; when He would win to salvation a sinful Samaritan woman, He bridged racial lines with love, denied Himself his needed physical rest, and talked with her of her soul's needs; when he would win an unscrupulous business man, he took time out from his touring to stop for dinner in that man's house, — and Zacchaeus received him gladly.

"And on a radiant morning, when the unbelieving disciples had fished all night and caught nothing, were tired and disheartened, he came and stood on the shore, beside a little fire of coals, with fish laid thereon — doing the *extra* thing, the thoughtful thing, careful to think of how hungry his tired fishermen would be — *That* is what He means when he talks about giving the cup of cold water . . .

"Imbedded in this verse is a many faceted diamond of truth, whose very surface reflects the Saviour Himself . . ."

A cup of *COLD* water . . . Beryl stopped abruptly. From The Nest had come a cry of distress, followed by a pounding noise, as if the old man were thumping on the floor with his silver-topped cane.

2.

SHE had set out in search of life. She found it quickly just
inside the vestibule of the morning — life and adventure,
and the beginning of a whirl of events that lifted her like a
tide lifting a rowboat, and swept her out and out toward new
horizons — and in the sweep, she recalled the poem by Tenny-
son which said:

> "I care not where His islands lift
> Their fronded palms in air;
> I only know I cannot drift
> Beyond His love and care."

Startled out of her story dream, she stood hesitant, listening. Again, she heard the sound — like the thumping of the
old man's cane upon the floor, or upon a piece of furniture,
and thought she heard also, a low cry of distress.

She moved quickly across the lawn to the latticed loggia
gate, went up the steps. The loggia was opened toward the
south also, and could be entered by any one of three arched
doorways, each with latticed gate like the one she had just
entered. At the right was a heavy oak door, closed, leading
perhaps into the living room of the house. On this closed
door she knocked, and waited only a brief moment, then she
lifted the latch, pushed, and followed the swinging door inside into a wide room furnished with easy chairs of rust
mohair, one of which faced the gray stone fireplace. In the
fireplace were cold black ashes only. Magazine racks, filled
with both books and magazines, occupied identical niches on
either side. She had a fleeting glimpse of French doors leading into a dining room, furnished with four box-seat, white-
oak chairs, trimmed in blue, arranged in order around a rectangular table of the same design, and in the exact center of
which, stood a blue, many-lipped glass bowl filled with arti-

ficial oranges, bananas and blue grapes . . . There was also a
stairway leading up, perhaps to the sun room on the roof.

For a bewildered moment, Beryl stood, then at the sound of
the old man's voice, she called, "Hello! Where are you?" and
followed her own voice into the room where he was.

She found him lying fully dressed, on a green studio davenport in a room to the left of the bath. The room itself was
furnished with office furnishings — desk, steel files, typewriter,
a library of much-used books. There was a pathetic look on
the old man's face, as he clung to his silver-topped cane, and
there was a vacant stare in his eyes. She knew that whatever
was wrong, whether real, or imagined, he was afraid.

"I — heard your motor," he said, — "*Quick!*" he wheezed.
"My heart —" He looked up at her, expectantly, as if her
white uniform was that of a nurse.

The word *quick* could mean anything, she thought. It could
mean, "Give me a heart stimulant!" "Get in touch with my
relatives!" It most certainly meant, "Do something — *anything!*"

If she *were* a nurse, she could give—. But she was not. She
was only a business college graduate, an employee in the law
office of spatulate-snouted Bailes Martini. She knew how to
write deeds and wills, how to prepare a lawyer's brief, to write
out insurance . . .

Beryl found herself going into action. Heart attacks did not
alarm her, for her own father had had many before the climactic one that had killed him. Father Lane had not been a good
invalid. He had been cross and exacting, and he had flouted
his invalidism in their faces at every responsibility that had
shadowed the household — "Well, what can *I* do about it!
I can't even provide for my own family! . . . Debts, debts,
debts! They drive me crazy! . . . Don't EXCITE me! The
doctor says I'll kill myself some day, losing my temper!"

And the doctor had been right. The poison continuously
released into the blood stream by worry and volcanic erup-
tions of wrath, had been too much, and the heart, erratic and

irritable, and the cause of his invalidism all those years, had
stopped . . .

Beryl found the old man's pulse, felt its strong, steady beat,
except for an occasional seeming "miss" which could be
caused by gas pressure, too much coffee, or perhaps by anemia.
It could be greatly aggravated by a feeling of alarm on the
part of the patient.

He seemed to relax when she took his wrist. She smiled at
him reassuringly. "Has someone been telling you your heart
is bad? Or have you been reading medical books?" She was
seeing her wizened little father, and thinking of how seriously his psychological twist had aggravated his condition. The
chief cause of Father's worry, she knew, had been a book on
heart diseases, meant by its publishers for the medical profession only. That book had been discovered in his room
after it was too late; too late because it had been read and re-
read, with many underscorings. It had so italicized itself in
his mind that every new symptom had been interpreted in
the doubtful light of the book . . .

"I had an examination a month ago, and I've been warned
to be careful." His explanation broke into her thoughts to
bring her back to the present. This, however, she was sure,
was not an attack, and yet he seemed to be afraid. She must
relieve his mind.

"I'll get you something to drink," she said. "What have
you in the kitchen? Tea would be good, if I don't make it
too strong."

He looked frightened again. "Don't leave me!" he begged.
"I'm not afraid to die, and I suppose I ought to have a doctor,
but —"

"You aren't going to die —"

Her words were like magic on his faith. He sighed, then
said, "I might. Old men do sometimes."

She turned, opened the loggia door to let in fresh air. She
must take away his fear, keep him calm until he could believe he was all right again. That, she knew from experience
with her father, would take time, but it would work wonders.

No need to let him bring on an actual attack by worrying. It could be done, she knew.

The air from the lake blew in crisp and cool, and was laden with the smell of seaweed and fish. That would revive him if anything would. Anyone who liked to fish as well as he —.

"Even if — if I am all right — now," he said, "I'm glad it happened. It showed me that the faith He has given me is strong enough to hold at a time like that. He had me singing, 'Have Thine Own Way, Lord.' Do you ever sing that song?"

"Sometimes."

He relaxed upon the pillow she brought for him. "Sing it for me, will you?"

She sang the first stanza softly.

When she finished, he lay studying her. "You're like my daughter," he said, adjusting his bifocals and frowning because he could not see better. "There's something about your voice —" He caught his breath, coughed a dry cough. His heart was "missing" again, and he relapsed into the former fear. He gestured toward the writing desk and the files. "Get a sheet of paper — in the first drawer. The desk pen is there. I want a codicil to my will. *Quick!*"

His *quick* exploded with such emotion that momentarily she herself was alarmed. She found paper and pen and came back. "Shall I call a doctor?" Her eyes circled the room in search of a telephone.

He shook his head impatiently. "If my time has come, it has come. Anyway, there isn't any telephone. We had it taken out when Elizabeth died —" He caught his breath again and ordered wheezily, "The will's the important thing now. You write it and I'll sign it."

And so she wrote, and in the writing felt her ears burning, and her own heart acting erratically because of the revelation the will contained . . . :

"I add this codicil to my will, written one month ago, which codicil is to make null and void the clause in that will bequeathing to my nephew, James Grabill, my Lake Crane estate —."

The old man stopped abruptly, coughed again, caught his breath spasmodically, while his eyes closed and his forehead drew itself into a worried pucker . . .

"*James Grabill!*" she thought. Was it possible that this old man was his uncle? This, then, was the foundation of all Jim's promises of great wealth. "Some day, Beryl, I'll be rich, so rich I'll be swimming in wealth. We'll see the world — old Mexico, Hawaii . . ."

"One more paragraph," the old man wheezed.

"Ready," she said, and wrote at his dictation:

"The order is to be reversed: The Nest and the Lake Crane estate is to go to my other nephew, Timothy, and the city property to James . . ." Again the old man stopped, closed his eyes as if debating something with himself, then he continued:

"And to Miss Beryl Lane, who at my request is writing this codicil, I bequeath the sum of five thousand dollars to assist her in her writing career . . . I do solemnly affirm that this is my last will and testament, and that it shall not be revoked."

To Beryl Lane, *five thousand dollars!* She was not hearing right! This could not happen to her. This was some crazy dream! . . . Jim, the old man's nephew?

Absently, unable to believe, she gave him the pen for his signature. She watched his trembling hand spell out the date and the name: JOHN SYLVESTER BISHOP.

As in a trance, she carried the codicil to the desk, blotted the ink, came back.

Suddenly the old man cried out sharply, raised himself upon an elbow. "Quick!" he rasped. "Hide it! There's someone coming! It might be my —"

There was the sound of a car in the drive at the side of the loggia. She folded the paper, thrust it into her bosom.

A young man in blue slack suit pushed open the car door, swept through one of the loggia gates and entered the living room. "Hello, Uncle John! Anybody home?" Then he saw Beryl and stopped short.

Beryl took one look and gasped, steadied herself against the desk and exclaimed, "JIM! What —?"

3

THE young man in the blue gabardine slack suit stopped in the living-room doorway, as aghast as the girl herself. His gray eyes and her blue ones met in what might have been conflict, if he had not been so surprised. He had expected to find only Old John, his uncle, *not* a strikingly attractive blond with flashing eyes that not only challenged his right to be here, but expressed a positive dislike for him.

"Not *Jim,*" he said smiling, "but *Tim!* And don't be alarmed. I won't cause any trouble — except that I'd like to know who you are, and why, and —"

The wizened old man on the studio davenport, broke in wheezily, "It's my heart. Miss — Nurse, I'd like you to meet my nephew —" He straightened up, peered quizzically through the tops of his glasses. "Which one are you? Jim, or Tim?"

The young man laughed, and said, "My eyes are gray."

"I'd like you to meet my nephew, Professor Timothy Grabill, of Phillips College — a twin to the Jim I mentioned in my —" Again the old man caught his breath, closed his eyes a second, coughed a dry cough. "Maybe you'd better get the doctor to be sure," he said. "Nurse tells me I'm all right, but —"

And that was the way it began . . .

Young professor Timothy Grabill, Ph.D., steered his maroon roadster through the winding forest trail toward the highway and the nearest doctor's office, not because a doctor was needed, but to satisfy old John's whim. And while he drove, he gave his thoughts to the new situation, and what to do about it — and about *her.*

A nurse! It was ridiculous, of course. Uncle John didn't any more need a nurse than the professor himself needed a wife — or wanted one. The professor was only twenty-seven, and there was plenty of time between that and forty, the age he had set for himself as soon enough to consider matrimony — if ever.

He had anticipated spending the summer vacation in nerve-building solitude, released from the strain of college classroom and the responsibilities that always weighed heavily upon the shoulders of an instructor. Also, he had planned to finish the manuscript of a new book, which this fall was to be used as a supplementary textbook in the philosophy department of which he was the head. With keen anticipation he had looked forward to swimming, motorboating and fishing, interrupted only by work on his book.

That challenge in the girl's eye —! She had called him *Jim!* She was, perhaps, another in the long parade of women who had lost their hearts — and their happiness — because of dashing, playboy Jim. How did she happen to be at The Nest? . . .

Yes, he could have finished his book easily. And the manuscript for it *must* be in the hands of the publishers at the earliest possible moment. To have his plans — and his mind — so completely upset at the very beginning of his vacation —. Well, he would see. Young Dr. Mahone, whose office he was headed for at this moment, would know how to convince Uncle John that there was nothing seriously wrong with his heart — nothing more than had been wrong with it for years — it was a bit irritable. The nurse would be dismissed, and the planned vacation would slide back into its groove and go spinning merrily along . . .

Planned . . . During the last hectic week of the school term he had wound up his own activities, gathered his little library of necessary reference works, his already bulky manuscript, his files of carefully indexed notes, packed them into his maroon roadster, and set sail for solitude.

"Isolation, thou art a jewel!" he had cried when the long nose of his car had turned in at the sign, lettered: "The Nest." He had been here many times before, and knew what silent thrills were in store. There would be the daily early-morning swim followed by two hours of concentrated, *uninterrupted* work in the sun room, while Uncle John traversed the lake, luring the walleye toward his creeping bait; after that, another plunge, and lunch; a nap and then the work of polishing sentences, checking and rechecking his work of the morning. There would be moonlit nights, when he would sit under the stars and dream; fishing trips, when the solitude he had always craved, and had always found time to have, would be his, in the environment he loved most. Sitting in the stern of old John's dinghy, the trusty little outboard motor put-putting gaily along, the prow of the dinghy pushing into the sunset, the wind in his face, the cry of the loon quavering across the water — being answered by a lonely mate from somewhere — Ah, it was going to be a summer, indeed . . .

The lake, this morning, when his car had followed the shore drive, had looked like a great blue-gold desert, stretching away and away toward the east, where the day's butlers were bowing in old rose uniforms to announce his majesty himself, the sun.

He had always been the dreamer. Jim and Tim were twins, yes, identical as far as physical features were concerned, with the one distinguishing exception — the color of their eyes. The one was a clear blue, like the blue of the sky, like those of the white-uniformed nurse . . .

Professor Grabill frowned at the comparison, stepped down on the accelerator and went back to his interrupted dream . . . The eyes of the other twin — of himself — were a mystic gray. Mystic was the word, he had been thinking, that described his psychological make-up. He was indeed the dreamer, the esthete, a lover of beauty and of artistic culture. He had admired true beauty whenever and wherever he had found it . . . There was beauty in character too, and in efficiency. There was a rugged beauty even in the gnarled old stumps of the basswood, which, in recent years because of the drouth, had died with the receding of the lake. And the Maker of beauty, to substitute for the loss of His basswood, had made new birches grow, where the waterline of the lake had used to be.

He was an efficient God . . .

That conception, he supposed, had come to him not only from the Book He had caused to be written in which He revealed Himself, but because of very efficient Jo Ann, his secretary at the college. Jo Ann worshipped God with all her heart and mind, and was the only woman who had ever made him look seriously over into matrimony's garden. Day before yesterday at the college, it had happened . . .

Jo Ann was busy at her desk in the adjoining room, typing chapter 10 of his new book, the title of which chapter was: "*The Law of Faith.*" He set his desk-pen in place, pressed the annunciator, and as always, like the rubbing of Aladdin's lamp, it produced the efficient Jo Ann, who, pencil poised, notebook in hand, stood, awaiting his pleasure.

He indulged in a faint smile and said, "Good Genie, wilt thou hasten to gather together in one, my manuscript to date, so that I may be on my way at the earliest possible moment tomorrow afternoon?"

She was small, dainty, semi-brunette, calm and efficient, groomed always to the nth degree of neatness — never a stray wisp of hair, or an over-dash of powder on her straight little nose. Her hazel eyes met his questioningly. He was only three years her senior, and without knowing that he was permitting his thoughts to stray, he thought that she would be not only efficient as a secretary but equally so as a home maker.

Because the time required to think such thoughts, was being paid for by the trustees of Phillips College, he called them in, like a hunter calling in his dogs when they were astray on a rabbit trail. He told her then, of his plans to finish the book at the Nest. This was neither the time nor the place to think of romance, nor was Jo Ann the girl to be at all interested. She was all secretary and business. She would never marry. She had been his secretary during his three years as instructor at Phillips. Their feelings for each other had never gone beyond propriety, and never would . . .

She turned at his dismissal and went back to her desk in the adjoining office. A moment later her typewriter keys were busy with page 127 of his manuscript — "To share is to gain, to withhold is to lose. 'Give and it shall be given unto you,' a Certain One had said long ago. Die and you shall live — and give life to others. The motive of true self-denial, which is a voluntary dying — and a new way of living — is *others*. Self-denial of itself is nothing, but motivated by love for others, it is everything. It is the living out of *His* Life within you — if indeed He be in you . . ."

He sat listening to Jo Ann's flying keys, and for a moment experienced a strange new emotion. He wondered why, and found no answer, except that he knew what she was typing and that his thoughts were following hers. There was a kindred feeling when sympathetic minds shared the same faith, and loved the same Person. That, he decided, was the beauty of marriage. Two, bound together in life's most sacred relationship, could hallow that relationship by a common faith . . .

His thoughts, as far as Jo Ann was concerned, had gone no farther, but had reached out instead to one, whom, as yet he knew he had not met, and who would, who must, awaken in him emotions deeper than admiration or comradeship. No woman had as yet done that to him — except of course in his adolescence, when his unschooled emotions had lied to him again and again, until he had learned never to believe them — and was a bachelor now because of it . . .

He swung his car over to the curb in front of Dr. Mahone's office, frowned at himself and his straying thoughts, when the very word doctor suggested "Nurse," and nurse suggested a white uniform, blue-buttoned all the way down in front, hair the color of old golden-rod, tucked into a blue snood. Hm! That wasn't a nurse's cap she had been wearing. Or was it? Didn't the girls on the campus at Phillips wear snoods? And weren't there many white, shark-skin dresses seen on the campus every day?

Oh, well, he wouldn't be bothered. Dr. Mahone would soon convince old John that he was well, and needed to eat something besides walleye pike; and the nurse, or whoever she was, would be sent on her way rejoicing. Too bad, though, if Jim had molested her. Or — maybe sent her here to take care of Uncle John, as a pay-off for having broken her heart . . .

One could never tell what Jim would do next — or who would suffer because of what he did.

4

YOUNG Dr. Mahone, listening to the steady thump, thump, thump of the old man's heart, with its seeming "miss" every now and then, — sometimes beating a full minute without irregularity, then skipping every fifth or sixth beat, — recognised the symptoms at once. He looked grave for a moment while he folded his stethoscope and put it into his bag, then he straightened up, and seeing the anxiety on the wizened old face, announced, "Your heart is quite strong, Mr. Bishop, a very good heart for one your age, but it's what the medical profession calls an irritable or an excitable heart. You haven't been catching any big fish lately?" he added jestingly.

Trustfully, the old man looked up into the smooth face of the doctor, with its miniature mustache making a dark shadow below the aquiline nose. "Not just lately, but there's a monster that hangs around just off the dock over on the other side." The blue eyes of the old man lit up with a fisherman's fire. "I'd planned to try him early this morning, but — Do you think it would be dangerous —?"

"The only danger would be to the fish," Dr. Mahone said. "You can live a long time yet if you take care of yourself — don't over-exert at any time; get plenty of rest and sleep, and go fishing often."

A little later, out on the loggia, he said to "nurse" and nephew, "There's nothing dangerously wrong, nothing you can't expect to go wrong with an old man's heart. His fear hasn't helped any, and you ought to keep him reassured. The main thing is not to let him overtax his strength. Keep him contented, tell him every day how well he looks, take the cream out of his coffee, and don't let him eat any flatulency-causing foods."

To Timothy Grabill, he added, "Better drive him in tomorrow for a blood check-up."

The doctor's car disappeared down the drive. The man in the blue slack suit and the girl in white shark-skin stood watching until he had been gone almost a full minute, then their eyes — his gray and her blue — met for the second time. Gray, always less expressive than blue or brown, seemed to her now like an old gray wall that cloistered some dark secret.

"Well?" the identical twin of Jim Grabill said, and saying it, she thought the gray was like the gray of a fire that had gone out. Once, during the doctor's examination she had seen him looking at her with eyes of admiration, but that fire now was dead.

The blue eyes did not flinch, but she heard in the quick breath that she *had* to take, the crackling of the folded paper in her bosom.

"We may as well find out who's who," he said, — a bit crisply, she thought, and thought also, how very much he was like his brother Jim; yet there was a gentleness in his voice that belied the rather stern look on his face — the same face in every detail as Jim's except for something deeper and more mysterious that was very plainly stenciled there.

"As soon as I look after my patient," she said. She turned and went into the house, and to the studio davenport where Uncle John lay.

"What do you think," the old voice wheezed, "is the doctor right? What did he say out there that he didn't want me to hear?"

She realized the truth, as she had guessed it before. Old John had one hundred percent faith in her, even above that of the doctor. He would believe whatever she said.

"The doctor is absolutely right. The only thing he told us out there was that you'd have to drink your coffee black, and that you couldn't have cabbage or cauliflower, but that you should get up as soon as you liked. He wants you out in the open, and to forget about your heart. Whenever it starts to act like a frisky colt, don't pay any attention to it, except of course, not to exert yourself. An irritable heart is like an irritable woman — it needs to be ignored. The more attention you give it, the worse it gets.

"The sun is up," she reminded him, "and I'll be needing a walleye for dinner. And now, I believe, your nephew and I are going to have an argument of some sort out on the dock." She turned to go, then remembered the codicil and came back. "What," she asked, "shall I do with this?"

He swung himself into a sitting position. His heart "missed" again, and he frowned. "If it would only stop acting crazy — Where's my nephew?"

"He's outside, at the dock, I think."

"You're sure?"

She looked out the window, saw him standing near the pergola, facing the lake. Then she turned back to John Bishop. His eyes squinted through the upper lenses of his bifocals at the paper in her hand.

"It'll have to be mailed to my lawyer," he said. "You take it over to your cottage when you go. I'll motor over this afternoon, and we'll fix up a letter. I don't want anybody to know, neither Jim nor Tim. They've been like Cain and Abel all their lives, not only in their dispositions but in their attitude toward revealed truth. Timothy is as gentle as Abel's lamb. He'd rather let Jim have everything than to cause any trouble. He wouldn't even hurt a fish — I — I forgot to set my minnow pail out into the lake last night. The sun'll warm the water and the minnows'll all be dead. I don't like to have minnows die like that —"

"They're all right," she told him. "I did it for you when I came over an hour ago."

Tim came in then, and with both of them supplying the old man with courage, he stood to his feet and hobbled out to the dock. Outside, the smell of the lake lifted his spirit. "I believe I *will* go after that walleye," he said. A little later, he was put-

putting down the shore, his fishing rod beside him, a widening trail of living silver following in the wake of his dinghy.

The two on the dock turned and walked back toward the rose-shaded pergola. She had left her notebook and pencil there. They sat down, facing each other across the white table.

He spoke first. "Of course you know I know you are not a nurse," he said.

"Of course."

"Then why did Jim send you here? — and where is Jim?"

"Jim didn't send me here — not knowingly. I'm here to get away from Jim. My cottage is over there across the bay, where I'm writing a book. I motored over this morning to get some local color, and a bit of fresh air before beginning the day's grind. I didn't expect to run into — all this. I had met your uncle a week ago when he stopped at my cottage with a fish. It seemed to be a case of love at first sight —." She smiled, raised her eyes to the gulls tossing above the dock. Their high pitched voices were in the minor, she thought.

The man with the gray eyes suddenly wanted to say, "I don't blame him." Instead, he said, "I've always liked to watch the gulls," and saying it, he felt he liked them better to-day because they were white — and because there was a sadness in their voices that matched the sadness in the blue eyes across the table from him. Their very movements were like the white rhythm of the music in this girl's personality. He had lived these twenty-seven years, and until to-day had not met the woman whose beauty was like this. That of so many women, the world over, displayed itself unctiously and seemed to say, "Here I am! What are you going to do about me — and *for* me?" The unbleached beauty of this girl said simply, "Here I am, and in a minute I'll be gone. Is there anything *I* can do for *you?*"

She went on with her story. "I was wearing white when he saw me, and for some reason he thought I was a nurse. It recalled to him his daughter, who, I believe he said used to be a nurse. Of course I told him I was a mere stenographer trying to write a book, but he likes to call me 'Nurse,' and I let him do it. I did nurse my father during his last illness, and he knows that. So, when I came this morning and heard him calling and pounding on the desk with his cane, — well, that's the story." She had told him everything except the part about the codicil. That, she decided, would have to wait until events untangled themselves — at any rate until she could untangle her own thoughts. She knew enough about will-making to know that in this state the codicil need not be attested by witnesses. The mere fact of its being written on a separate piece of paper would make no difference, if it were properly signed.

The gray eyes across the table were studying her intently. "You came to get away from my brother, Jim?" he asked.

She nodded, reached for her notebook and started to rise. He put out his hand. "Wait," he said. "I've never been a father confessor, but if there's anything I can do — or say, or if there's anybody I have to kill —" He was jesting, of course, but he had heard enough of Jim's escapades, had seen too much wreckage, and had helped to clear away some of it. He had come to the end of the rope, as far as patience with Jim was concerned.

She was standing now, looking across into his eyes, that were so gray, into the face that was so identical with Jim's, yet so much more gentle and — refined. His was like the sermon of that morning — and Jim's was like the picture of some of the movie stars she saw in advertisements: handsome and daring and — *retouched*. Without the photographer's legerdemain, they would reveal themselves as they were. But she had seen Jim *un*retouched . . .

They were interrupted then by another slack-suited young man, who came swinging down the path from a neat little cottage farther up the shore. In a moment he was there, and was introduced to Beryl as Mr. Hartford Sprague. The Spragues — Hartford, and his Geneveve — were caretakers of the estate, Beryl learned. They cooked the old man's meals, and looked after things in general.

"You must come up to the cottage for breakfast," Sprague said. "My Jenny has everything ready. I see Mr. Bishop is out with his dinghy."

She would have liked to stay, but she decided against it. Some other time, perhaps. Just now she wished to be alone somewhere to think things through, and to untangle her thoughts which had knotted themselves into grotesque figures and shapes . . .

"My work is calling me," she said, "and I must be getting back."

Timothy Grabill followed her out to the dock, steadied her boat while she stepped in and took her place in the stern. Then he unleased the anchor rope from the dock post, and gave her boat a shove. He watched it glide out into the deeper water, watched her turn the prow about with the oar, then he called, "Don't forget that you are a nurse, — and come back to look after your patient." When, a little later, her boat was riding the waves far out, he was still standing and watching, and thinking as he watched.

5.

THE lady pilot, her left hand on the rubber grip of the steering handle of her outboard motor, the wind in her face, bits of spray catching in her autumn leaf hair, her rowboat's prow parting the waves, felt herself being swept along into a strange future, dark with mystery, yet lighted with new light.

She had seen in Timothy Grabill, the one thing lacking in his identical twin, Jim. Jim was a photo retouched; Timothy did not need retouching. He was as he was: genuine.

Her emotions at this moment were like the ingredients of a cake during the mixing process, and there seemed to be a Power from above, stirring, adding more of this and of that, always stirring. By and by she would be "all in a piece," but until then she did not know even herself. She had once loved Jim Grabill; she had now come to hate Jim Grabill — not the man, but the things that made him what he was; today she had seen him as he ought to be, and as she knew he must be before she could love him again — and yet he was not the same, but another.

From the little purse in the seat beside her, she drew a mirror and studied her face, and saw behind her the blue-suited man standing on the dock in front of the Nest. She saw the deep blue color in her own eyes, the color enhanced no doubt by the blue of the lake and sky. Far down the shore she saw the old man's dinghy, creeping along. He sat in the stern, stooped and immobile, but she knew he was content with the deep contentment known only to men who loved the lake as he did.

"*. . . my last will and testament . . .*" He was driving over this afternoon to dictate a letter to his lawyer. At that time, the codicil could be copied by him in his own writing.

She must hurry back to her manuscript now, not permit the things that were happening to her to seem more important than events in her story. Or was the whole thing merely a story, and she herself the story-book heroine, the Cinderella-girl?

When she reached her own side of the bay, Sam Grady, the caretaker, came down to the dock to help her beach the boat. The Gradys were good neighbors, and had, upon her arrival a week ago, taken her into their hearts.

"Up early again, I see," Grady said, his voice booming sonorously. In size he was little less than a gorilla. Mrs. Grady, who at this moment stood in gingham apron at her veranda door, waved a plump arm in welcome.

The boat beached, and Grady on his way to another errand, Beryl walked the sloping board walk to her own porch entrance. It was a bare little cottage, built only for summer use. The walls were unfinished, and the partitions between rooms typical of lake cottages the country over; but in it was privacy, and to her it was a house of creation, for here her book manuscript should be born. Here she was giving of her very self in its production.

In her room now, she read and re-read the strange codicil. It could not be true; and yet it was true. There it was, in her own handwriting. Five thousand dollars would pay off the mortgage on the old home, free her from slavery to Martini, send Larry off to college, take the stoop out of Mother's shoulders and spirits. She herself would be free to follow the career of her choice. Nothing now could stop her.

She stored the folded bit of paper in her file where she kept her manuscript, locked the drawer, commanded her emotions to be subject to her will, and sat down to write. At ten o'clock she went to the camp office for the mail. There were two letters awaiting her. The one from home was in Mother's handwriting:

"My dearest Beryl:

"Your letter gave us all a thrill, and made us a bit envious too, I suppose, for it was ninety-eight in the shade here yesterday and the humidity was stifling. This week, especially, has been hard, for we've been canning berries and apples, and my nerves almost went to pieces.

"And now, after that bit of pessimism, I wish to be a little more cheerful. The thought of which you wrote in your letter about doing the *extra* thing, giving the cup of *cold* water, is beautiful. I don't know how I've happened to miss it all these years, but I have. Thank you so much, dear Beryl, for telling me about it. I'm sure it will brighten things a bit around the home. Larry thinks it 'scrumptious,' as he says, and you should see the way he plays it up. If I can get Dora Jeanne to adopt it, it will save her many a heartache, and eliminate a lot of family friction.

"Do pray for Dora Jeanne, Beryl. She is at that age, you know, when nothing is right with the world, and she is believing herself to be a martyr. Also she still has visions of finding a young gallant who will carry her away. No home responsibilities for her when she marries, she says. No household drudgery. It's getting to be quite a problem, and she sometimes threatens to leave home.

"Tell me more about this Mrs. Schaeffer. She must be a very gracious person, but it seems too much like a dream that she should single you out of all the rest of the world. I am not so sure I would have advised you to accept her offer, but now that you have done so, we can only hope for the best. Yet, Beryl, you must fortify your heart and mind against a possible failure, for the higher the ambition, the greater the disappointment in case of failure.

"I used to have my dream too, Beryl. I wanted to write — I wanted to paint — I wanted to travel — I wanted to fling my name across the world's sky in letters of gold. Instead, I married and became a mother, chained to routine and poverty. Only the love of Christ kept me from going insane, I think. And it was His love that gave you to me, to chase away the gloom.

"But I would not shatter your dreams, Beryl. Perhaps mine came short of fulfillment, that yours might come true. Always it is that way —: The tree is hewn down, or else it falls in a storm, and from its roots new life springs up, and lifts its head high — as high at any rate, as the mother tree — *for awhile*. And then the next generation . . .

"Thank you very much for the check. Be sure you are not neglecting your own needs. Write again soon.

"With much love,

"Mother"

The other letter was from Mrs. Schaeffer herself. Beryl read it with leaping heart.

"My dear Beryl:

"I don't know of anything that has caused me more genuine joy than this little investment I am making in His Name. Even if it should fail, I shall have had the joy of giving the cup. I think I'd been serving luke-warm water all my life, until I met you. I professed Christianity when I was only a little girl, but I had been so wrapped up in myself and how much I could be blessed, that I found no genuine joy in service. Always it was the blessings I was after. I went to hear this man, or that one, always seeking a new blessing, by *receiving*. Now I know — and you have taught me — that blessings continue to come to him who passes them on — they enter in while we are giving them out to others . . .

"I have reread your story in the magazine, and I am more convinced than ever of your ability. Not only so, but of the strange power in what you write. Others may write with equal skill, and perhaps with as colorful phrasing, but your writing has *soul* . . .

"I enclose your check a day or two in advance. Remember you are in my employ now — and that I am having the time of my life doing this little bit. And oh, how giving the cup of cold water *warms* my own heart! . . . I have not lost my reward — and some day you and I — and the minister who first preached the sermon, illuminating that precious old passage in the Book, will have our multiplied reward. Around the world, and in many languages, Christian people will catch the meaning of the Master's words, and results that will astonish the Church beyond all measure, will follow.

"Just to show you how the cup of *cold* water satisfies, listen to this: A week ago I was compelled to take lunch out. I went to the little Pearl Cafe, where you and I first met. The waitress there, the one with the large rings under her eyes, sighed a little wearily when she came to my table. My first impulse was to be impatient with her for hanging sigh-clouds over my booth. Instead, I offered sympathy and found out that she had a husband in the hospital, and a sick baby. *Luke-warm* water would have been to offer sympathy only. *Cold* water required that I do something extra. Too busy to do something *extra,* unless I sacrificed a visit to the art museum to see a special painting in which I was interested, I cancelled the art exhibit, and when the dear girl was off at two o'clock, I drove her home in a cab. There I found the rent unpaid. I paid it. I found the baby needed a doctor. I called one. I arranged for a maid to take care of the baby while the mother is at work. I discovered the grocer had refused to let them have credit any longer, because he couldn't afford to — or thought he couldn't. I paid the bill, and two or three others.

"Reward? Too much, almost, to believe. But Sunday morning that little mother came to church, with the baby in her arms, and when the invitation was given for souls to be saved, she arose, and marched humbly to the altar, carrying her baby with her . . .

"So, dear Beryl, this thing works. It will always work. It will do something to the Church everywhere, if they know and practice it. So I am praying for you as you write. I *know* you can do it. You *will* do it. I'm making the check larger this week, because you may wish to send a bit more to your mother.

> "With much love,
>
> "Beulah Schaeffer."

There were tears in Beryl's eyes when she finished the letter. It seemed too much to believe that it was happening to her, yet it was true. She returned each letter to its envelope, walked to the front door and out onto the porch. From far across the lake, now tossing nervously in the rising wind, came the cry of a loon, quavering like a night owl's eerie wail. Yonder, beached at the dock, was the old man's dinghy. She turned and went back into the cottage, closing the door after her, and there on a grass rug, she knelt to pray. And in the prayer which came from a bewildered, yet impassioned heart, she said, among other things . . . "If it be Thy will for me that I climb no higher than a secretary's position in Martini's office, Thy will be done . . ." Praying, the Spirit Who indwelt her, stirred into white heat her ambition's fire, that she might write only at His dictation, that those who should read might be given winged feet to go and go and go with the gospel and that those who went might learn the secret of doing the extra thing — the unexpected thing, which, by its very unexpectedness, might capture the hearts of unbelievers and win them to Christ.

From her knees she moved as one in a trance to her typewriter, and filled with the Spirit, as Peter of old was filled on the days of Pentecost, she wrote until it was past the noon hour. The characters who played in the word-waves of her story became living human beings, more real to her, more vital and necessary to her happiness than Jim Grabill or his identical twin, or Martini or Mrs. Schaeffer, or even her mother and Dora Jeanne and her only brother, Larry.

After a refreshing siesta in the hammock on her cottage veranda, she changed to play togs and went down to the lake.

The Gradys had taught her the art of fishing, how to run the outboard motor, and the most favorable feeding places for the different kinds of fish. From the very first time she had felt the thrill of a fish on her line, she had loved the sport. Already she was believing herself to be expert, especially in casting for bass. The old man preferred trolling for walleye, but that was his privilege.

This was all a part of the arrangement with Mrs. Schaeffer. The little cottage was furnished, rent free, all expenses paid; outboard motor, boat, and other recreational facilities provided . . .

And now, here she was, in Mrs. Schaeffer's modest summer resort, *The Spruces,* doing the thing which all her life she had dreamed of doing, and in preparation for which she had done much more than dream. As a girl she had read and studied a thousand percent more than was required to pass from one grade to another in school. In those school days, poems in red ink had flown on faltering wings to magazine editors, had flown back again with rejection slips — and had made round trips to other editors. Fiction, too, had done the same. It was only in the past year that an occasional manuscript had found favor in an editor's eyes, and by the alchemy of the printing press, been multiplied and sent out to ten thousand readers — in the same way a little lad's lunch, one day, had been multiplied by the Master's hands into enough to feed five thousand men — only *His* was miracle. But could He not take the truth that she was weaving now into her story, and by a miracle of His Grace, give to eat, five thousand times five thousand . . . ?

"You must fortify your heart and mind against a possible failure . . ."

Mother was right, of course. She must not hope to reach the whole world, but only to be used as an instrument in the Master's hand to reach those who would not otherwise be reached. She would be only one of His branches; He Himself was the Vine, without Him she could do nothing — everything she might do *without Him* would *be* nothing, for it would not be nourished by love.

Five thousand dollars!

The old man had said he would motor over in the afternoon, but he had not come. The whole thing seemed like a dream, and only the codicil in her file proved that it was actually happening.

It was recreation time now. The lake in the afternoon, just before twilight, was calm again, as it was so often at this hour. She knew a place far around the lake where bass fishing was said to be good. The old man had told her yesterday.

Beautiful, beautiful world. Her boat rounded the point on her own side of the lake, swung back at a slow angle and followed the shore line into the west. Here were many cottages, some more artistic than others. Summer homes for the wealthy were built in places like this. Beryl throttled her motor down to a trolling speed, and as the shore crept slowly past, she entered into this world of affluence, where the rich played and danced and motored — and were unhappy. She knew they were unhappy, most of them, for they were always *grasping*, rather than *giving*. And He Who knew all things had said, *"It is more blessed to give than to receive."*

There were great houses now, of American and Colonial architectural types; great rolling lawns that sloped down to sandy beaches; wide, white docks extending far out into the water where motor- and sail-boats were moored. Roses climbed vari-shaped trellises, winding footpaths lured into shaded nooks; luxurious cars stood parked on paved drives beside equally luxurious homes . . .

Out-door furniture of many colors ornamented the spacious lawns, which, Beryl thought, were as fresh and as neatly kept as the watered greens on golf courses . . .

Here, speed-boats shot at angles across the lake, roaring, leaving turbulent water trails behind, sending long, high swells speeding toward the docks and the shore . . .

These people, Beryl thought, knew nothing of the drab routine of the working classes. These were the descendants of those who, in a past generation, had worked, and saved, and invested, — perhaps. If these, who had so much, would yield allegiance to Him who gave His all, — but they would never do that, not all of them. Here and there He would find a Mrs. Schaeffer who would do His will . . .

These, too, were those who had time to read, who yearly waded through millions of words which clothed so nakedly the stories of the world. If these would read her book . . .

The sun was touching the horizon in an open place between wooded hills, when she reached the bass fishing waters. She shut off the alert little motor, took the oars and rowed silently toward the lily pads near the shore. Softly, oars dipping into smooth water, she sat tense and expectant. In another moment . . .

She swung her casting rod in a quick, swift arch; the plunker sailed through the air, struck the water with a resounding whack. She reeled in, while the plunker fought its way toward the boat, following the minutest dictates of her skilled right hand . . .

The first bass struck ten feet from the boat; the second, two minutes later, at the very moment her lure hit the water. Beryl thrilled to the joy of it, and thought with pity of people who giggled dizzily over cocktails at two o'clock in the morning, swilled down seltzers at eight, dragged through dull days with headaches, and knew so little of life's cleaner thrills . . .

Behind her, its motor silent, a white dinghy rounded the point of land. A skilled oarsman rowed with silent-dipping oars toward her fishing grounds . . .

She did not hear him coming and did not know he was there until she heard the singing of a reel and saw the splash his plug made as it struck the water at the edge of the lily-pads.

6.

THEY rode back in the moonlight, both in his dinghy, towing her own boat behind. There was a law against boats being on the lake at night without a light, he said, and she had brought none. He put her in the wide seat directly in front of him — and facing him — and let her hold the flashlight. Behind them her white rowboat was dark under the pale moon — pale because it was dying. It would be born again in three days and expand nightly until in a few weeks it would be full. The lake at night would be beautiful then, he said.

They talked of things in common: of the book she was writing, and of the one he hoped to finish before the summer should pass; of fishing; of college — her business college and his professorship. They talked of books and authors, and finally of Jim Grabill.

"We've been everything to each other but brothers," Timoothy Grabill said, his voice sounding so much like Jim's that it startled her. Once, on a similar night, she had ridden with Jim on a lake nearer the city. That night Jim had proposed marriage, had promised many things, and before the evening had passed had made love with passionate pleadings. "Some day I'll be rich, and you can forget you're Martini's slave, in the whirl of fun you and I'll be having at the very top of the ladder . . ."

That night Jim had gone away in a huff because she had spurned his proposal. He had come back the next night, repentant. There had been several months of Jim, and then, at last, she had recovered from the delirium which had made her incoherent in her thinking. . . . Jim's wealth could have saved her from Martini, and it could have delivered Mother from poverty. She had considered that too, and had tried to make herself believe she loved him.

In the meantime she had found a church where the riches of the Word were unfolded, and there had yielded her life fully to Him who is the Way, the Truth, and the Life. There she had heard the sermon that since had become the theme of her life, and to marry Jim had seemed inconsistent. To her now, he belonged only to the past.

Tonight, her hand clinging to Timothy Grabill's powerful flashlight, watching the little moon over his shoulder, wondering what he might be thinking, — O, this was the life! What was that he had said a moment ago? He and Jim had been everything to each other but brothers?

"He is not wholly to blame," Tim went on. "After high school he decided to take up pharmacy. He chose the state university for that, and I went to a small college on the coast — a new college, whose reputation was yet to be earned but which paid no salaries to agnostic professors to destroy the faith of its students . . .

"You know," Timothy Grabill said philosophically, "a man *is* very much what he *knows*. And if what he knows is distorted or untrue, or if it is without God, then the man is — like that. I shouldn't want you to think too hard of Jim, for that reason."

"I shan't," she said.

The conversation turned to Uncle John. "He is becoming more and more forgetful," Tim said, "especially since Elizabeth died. They've spent their summers here at the lake for years. He built the Nest two years ago. Originally they lived in the cottage where the Spragues are now. Uncle John seems to like the old cottage best, but it reminds him too much of his Elizabeth, so he seldom goes up there any more. Elizabeth was drowned in the lake in front of the dock there, about a hundred feet out . . ."

There was more about Uncle John and his "heart attack."

"He's been a little short of breath for several years, but his doctor in the city tells him he's good for a long time if he is careful not to overdo. Of course we know he is an old man, and he knows it too, but he can't seem to remember it.

"I think he'll be more careful after this morning. He was really frightened. I suppose, though, it was only a normal fear which would be common to most of us, if we thought we were dying — even though we knew we were going — home."

They talked of different things, and all the time she was liking the man in the stern of the boat better and better, liking his voice, his gentleness, his thoughtfulness . . .

"Here's a bottle of mosquito lotion," he said, fishing it out of his tackle-box. "The little ladies are vicious this time of night."

She liked his humor also.

"Ladies?" she asked.

"Science has only recently discovered it. It is the female mosquito which bites. They have to have blood for reproductive purposes."

"That sounds more like a philosophical remark than a scientific one," she told him. "Somewhere I've read that philosophy is knowledge that explains facts; whereas science is exact knowledge. . . . You are a professor of philosophy, I believe—?"

They laughed, and she liked his laugh.

It was eight-thirty when they docked at her beach. "If you wouldn't mind a little spin on the lake without such a wooden chaperone," he said, gesturing carelessly toward her rowboat, "I'd like to have you run over with me for a fish-fry. The Spragues are expecting me at the cottage, and one extra plate won't matter. They're always comfortably informal."

She hesitated. Every new experience was fuel for her story fire. She was reminded also that Uncle John had not driven over today as he had promised. He had forgotten, perhaps. It seemed to her now that she ought to explain everything to Timothy.

"Wait till I run in and change," she said and hurried up the board walk to her cottage. Grady came puffing over with apologies when she reached her veranda. "Sorry I didn't hear you coming," he said.

Timothy came then and there were introductions and explanations, enough of the latter to satisfy both Sam Grady and his plump little wife, who were also recipients of Mrs. Schaeffer's cold water, and had specific instructions to watch over Beryl as they would a precious jewel. Mrs. Schaeffer had found the Gradys as she had the weary waitress in the cafe, and assuring herself that they were worthy and capable, and needing a caretaker at The Spruces, had given the cup.

In her cottage, Beryl searched in her files for the folded bit of paper, tucked it into a topper pocket, slipped the topper on over her dress and in a few moments was ready.

"Good girl," Timothy said, when she came out and they were walking down the dock to his dinghy, "putting on warm clothing without having your mother here to tell you."

He seated her as before, facing the stern. In passing, his hand touched her shoulder; that was all. She felt the touch and was stilled by it; and all the way across the lake she was aware of it. She told herself to the rhythm of the waves and the roar of the motor, that a new and strange future was about to dawn for her. This courteous twin brother to Jim Grabill was going to capture her heart in one swift rush of time.

There were other things to think about also. There was the codicil in her topper pocket, bequesting to her five thousand dollars, and to Timothy Grabill the beautiful Lake Crane estate, and all property adherent thereto.

All this, she thought, had been offered to her by one who now would never come into its possession. If she had married Jim —!

And if I should marry Timothy . . .! She erased the thought. It did not belong in her life story.

The lake, tonight, lay under the stars and the tiny slice of white moon like a field of green wheat rolling in the wind. She would be glad to meet Hartford Sprague's "Jenny"; especially glad to spend another hour with Tim, *Professor* Timothy Grabill! She could not think of him as that. Never before had she met a college professor so young and so serenely surren-

dered to the inflow of life from the Vine. . . . And, without trying to be, he was so graciously romantic.

At that very moment he was saying, "I am more and more
convinced of one thing, and that is that a truly-born-again
believer in Christ is actually united to Him in a mystical union
as real in the spiritual realm as the branches of a vine are
united to the vine itself. 'I am the true Vine,' the Saviour
said. That being true, we have within ourselves the same kind
of life that He has. It is the inflow of the life of the vine that
gives life to the branch, and it is His life within us which en-
ables us to bear fruit. He tell us so in the fifteenth chapter of
John. It is through us He is able to manifest Himself to others. In me He has a voice in the college classroom; in you, a
voice through the printed page, in the office, everywhere He
sends you . . ."

They stopped at the Nest first. They found the old man
with a book in front of the fireplace. He looked up at them
through the tops of his bifocals, and seeing Beryl, shuffled to
his feet, a seamed forefinger marking the place in the book
where he had been reading.

"And how is my patient tonight?" she asked.

"One hundred percent," he said, — "Here, draw up chairs.
Bring the wicker from the study, Tim."

It was too bad to disappoint him. "We stopped in to say
'Good-night'," Tim explained. "We're having a fish-fry over
at the cottage. I may be out a bit late, but I have my pass-key.
Everything all right?"

The book, Beryl noticed, was the same that had lain in the
stern of the dinghy this morning.

"Wait," the old man requested, "listen to this from Simpson. It's the most beautiful thing I've read —"

He carried the book to the table lamp and read to them a
paragraph. Interlocking with the thing Timothy had said a
few moments ago on the lake, it was a precious thing to hear.
There was contentment on the old man's face as he rasped
out the beautiful words:

"The Holy Spirit was to become corporately united and identified with the life of a believer, so that He would bring us into direct personal union, and act not upon us but *in* and *through* us, becoming part of our very life, controlling every faculty, volition, and power, from the inmost depths of our being. . . . The sunshine enters into the midst of the flowers and manifests itself in all the living beauties and tints of the blossoms. . . . The water saturates the ground and comes forth again in the leaf, and laden fruit. . . . These are but distant approximations to the blessed mystery that the Holy Spirit as a Person enters into the life and being of a consecrated disciple and controls every choice, affection, thought and action, and fulfills his own promise, 'I will dwell in you and walk in you.' . . ."

When they were about to leave, the old man called Beryl to come back. Timothy waited for her in the loggia.

The expressive blue eyes of the old man were looking steadily into hers. "You haven't said anything to anyone?"

"No, I haven't."

"I was going to drive over today, but I must have forgotten." He frowned. "It's very humiliating, being an old man." For a moment he seemed to be debating with himself. "Tell me. Did you have freedom in writing today? What happened this morning didn't upset you?"

"Not at all. In fact, it seemed to help. It's quite a shock, of course, to find myself an heir to a lot of money. I— "

He turned to the table lamp, stooped, held the book low. "Here's something you must weave into the story. I have it marked — let me see. Here it is —" He stumbled against the chair, balanced himself unsteadily, and came to a sitting position on the wide overstuffed arm. . . "Awkward old man," he grumbled to himself, and then he tilted his head and read to her through the lower lenses of his bifocals: " 'The Holy Spirit, God's medium for the revelation of spiritual realities, brings Christ from the throne, until distance is annihilated and space has no power to divide . . .' "

"Beautiful," she said, when he finished.

"Do you think you can use it? People need to know that more than anything else. . . . You can go now. Tomorrow I'll motor over, and we'll — you know. I think maybe I'll wish to make a change or two."

A little later Timothy and Beryl were out on the lawn walking toward the beach. "Tell me," he said, as they turned into the footpath leading up to the cottage, "How do you so completely capture a man's heart in such a short time —? Uncle John's, I mean?"

"Have I?"

"Irrevocably. You should have heard him talk after you had gone this morning, that is, when he had come back from his fishing."

"And of course, you argued against him."

"I was neutral. I don't go blind so easily."

On bantering ground, they could say things which, were they said seriously, might quicken pulses and send them spinning on the road to romance. And yet, she asked herself, was she not *thinking* seriously! *Too* seriously?

They stopped for a moment, looked back toward the Nest, white under the moon. They could see the shadow of the old man as he sat beside the fire.

"He's the dearest old man I ever met, I think," Beryl said.

The lake below them lapped softly against the rocks, which a little farther on, at the foot of a stairs leading down from the Sprague's cottage, were piled in a great jagged heap.

He took her arm gently, felt its firm warmth through her topper sleeve and steered her up the path to the cottage.

With that firm hand upon her arm Beryl was aware of a feeling of contentment. It was a hand she could trust. He was a friend she would be proud to have. Knowing him would make it easier to write the tremendous truths of her book. He was like the hero of her story: refined, intelligent, in love with her Saviour.

————

"Supper" with the Spragues was a merry time. Beryl learned that they were graduates of Phillips College, and had been scheduled to sail as missionaries for Ethiopia when the war closed the door there. They had found a pastorless church six miles up the highway in a little Finnish settlement, and Hartford preached there every Sunday morning. He and his Geneveve were on the second year of their honeymoon which, they said, would last forever.

She was a vivacious little thing, Beryl thought, with trilling laughter and expressive blue eyes that were only for her husband. She fixed toasted cheese sandwiches and served them with long, white steaks of walleye. The four made a game of the dishes afterward, then sat in the living room before a log fire, and played a new word-meaning game, an improvement on the once popular game of Anagrams, in that it required more skill. It would appeal, Beryl thought, especially to those who were literary minded.

As in the game after which it was patterned, words might be "borrowed" from an opponent's list, if by adding a letter or letters to it, a new word could be formed. Once during the game, Beryl borrowed the word "love" from Timothy's impressive array of words, and added the letter "r".

"You stole my love," he accused her, and like a school girl she blushed and hated herself for it. But he seemed not to have noticed.

After the game, they sat on the wide veranda and watched the saucer moon until it dropped into the lake. They seemed to belong to each other, somehow, these four. Beryl thought she had never seen a happier couple than the Spragues, or a more hospitable. Once, when a cloud hid the moon for a moment, she saw him steal a kiss, and whisper a nothing, which, Beryl knew, was *everything*. Love like that would be wonderful. Love would never have been like that with Jim Grabill. And she would always have had to wonder, when he was away, if he might find another woman who would capture his fancy; and whether his lips had kissed others while he was gone. Love *could* be beautiful, if it were like this. And later, when children should come, and sickness too, — which always came at some time or other —, if love reigned, there would be triumph. Should life threaten to become routine, and the struggle for existence smother the fire of love, it could be rekindled by the doing of the "extra" thing, the surprising thing, the courteous. Love that lasted did not have to start with an explosion, nor carry enough fuel to keep it burning forever. It could begin with a very small fire, and it could be fed with such little things — things that might otherwise be wasted.

If love ever truly comes to me, it will have to be like that — like this . . .

They talked of the war that raged on another continent, and which was reaching out long economical tentacles to take in the whole world. They talked, too, of the world's missionary program, and of how in spite of the war, more Bibles were being sold — and read — than before. Many doors were being closed, but those that remained open, were "great doors, and abundant," and multitudes, in their extremity, were being saved.

And if, when the war was over, the victors did the "extra" thing, the thing not considered deserved, the over-and-above thing, a *future* war might be prevented . . .

It was Beryl who offered this last, and it was accepted as "right," even if it might never be crystalized.

"The heart of man is desperately wicked," Geneveve said, quoting from the Bible.

"Deceitful and desperately wicked," Hartford added.

"Which," the professor offered, "is the cause of all war, all crime. Sin in the heart is the root of the whole thing. Our Lord says in Mark seven, verses twenty-one and twenty-two: 'For from within, out of the heart of men, proceed evil thoughts, adulteries, fornications, murders, thefts, covetousness, wickedness, deceit, lasciviousness, an evil eye, blasphemy, pride, foolishness . . .' "

And Sprague said, "The new birth is the only solution to the sin problem. A new nature, God created and implanted within a man, has always been His method . . ."

While they talked, thoughts and ideas for tomorrow's writing played about the theme of Beryl's story like a school of fish about an attractive lure.

"Well, there goes the moon," Tim said when its lower corner touched the lake. "We'd better be taking the lady of the lake home."

They all went down to the dock together, and Tim drove her across.

At her own dock he made her remain seated until he had beached the dinghy, then he took her hand, and guided her toward the prow. The thing that happened then was so unexpected that neither of them could have prevented it. He himself may have been to blame, he thought. In any event, if he had not been thinking of the way she had blushed when she had stolen his "love" — he, a college professor, immune to romance all these years! — if it had not been so dark —

But it was so dark, with the moon gone, and he *had* been remembering her crimson cheeks, how very pretty they were — autumn leaf hair, columbine cheeks: old golden rod and ripe peach . . .

Anyway, it happened. Her foot caught in the anchor rope and she fell — where a woman was supposed to fall when there was a man near-by. Oh, she would not have *fallen* — not actually. He knew it afterward. They both knew more afterward. They were both much wiser.

A brief moment later they were on the dock, apart, and a little short of breath, with only his hand guiding her arm as they went up the board walk to her cottage.

He waited on the veranda while she turned on the lights and until she came back. He was glad the Gradys lived next door, for it was not good for a young woman to live alone at a lake cottage, not in a world that knew not God. The Gradys' porch light was on, he noticed.

"I'm perfectly safe here," she told him when she came back, as if in answer to his thoughts. "My sleeping room is next to theirs, and if a burglar should wish to risk his reputation by attempting to rob the poor, I could scream for help and get it in a flash. Isn't he a gorilla, though?"

"There are giants in *these* days," he said.

"And I can scream like a loon. Besides, I was brought up on the farm. I have muscles —" They were just talking, she knew, both of them wishing the evening had only begun. They would see each other again — *when?*

In his thoughts he was still back in the dinghy, steadying himself, steadying her. It was time to go now, however. He touched his hat in a courteous gesture and said, "Thank you for a very pleasant evening, Miss Lane. There's no reason why we shouldn't have a little spin on the lake tomorrow — in the afternoon, perhaps — is there?"

They decided on three o'clock. He would drive over in Uncle John's dinghy, and they would explore an island he knew about far up toward the head of the lake.

He turned and went down the walk, shoved off, and a little later was steering toward the light at the end of the dock in front of the Nest.

In the dark, steering toward the light. Young Professor Graybill admitted it at last. He was on his way out. In one short day he had traversed the whole labyrinth of love, had met his lady in every avenue; every avenue opened into another — and she was also there. And now, tonight, unwittingly as far as she was concerned, she had taken his hand and led him out.

His hand on the rubber grip on the steering handle of his outboard motor still felt the touch of her hand. Philosopher, he admitted her grace and physical charm, but these were not the cause of the lightness of his heart. There was such a thing as soul, — intellect, emotion, will — all intertwined with beauty.

He had gone blind quickly. *And he had found his sight!* The lightness of his heart was also heaviness, as if he were punished for having played out of tune so long. Philosopher Emerson had once written, "The right punishment for one out of tune, is to make him play in tune . . ." The punishment itself was pleasurable.

Under the spell of his illusion, he docked his boat, followed the bobbing trail of his flashlight toward the stoop of the loggia. Inside, in the living room, long lazy flames from the fireplace tossed their shadows upon the orange colored walls, upon the closed French doors of the dining room, upon the mohair overstuffed chairs.

He seated himself in the chair to the left of the fire, listened for the customary heavy breathing of Uncle John, which, were he asleep, could be heard in any adjoining room.

"Like a log, as always," Timothy chuckled, and pressed the switch of the little radio at his side, manipulating the dial so the program would be barely audible. He wanted the late news and the weather forecast. For upon the weather depended the mood of the lake and it was going to be very necessary for him to cross over tomorrow — and the next day and the next. In the weeks ahead, there would be bass-fishing trips, fish-fries at the Cottage, long drives in his car, or in Uncle John's dinghy, touring the lake. And, some evening, they would take his pressure-gas-camp-stove, find a beach far away, and there learn to know each other more intimately, explore each others' minds,—

The weather report was coming in now — a little statically, — for tomorrow — *"High winds, followed by thunder showers . . ."*

Oh, well, he could drive around the lake in his car, after working hours. *Working* hours! He had forgotten about his book. Well, he had better go back out to the dock, pull the dinghy far up on the sand, and turn it bottom side up, or the waves and the rain would fill it. He would detach the outboard motor also, and bring it in rather than leave it out as was old John's habit, when he was planning a fishing trip early the next morning . . .

Stars hung in the sky like lights in a canopy of blue steel. There was scarcely a breath stirring, and as yet there were no clouds, but off to the west, where the moon had hung an hour ago, lightning played, and there was the low rumble of thunder.

He caught the boat's prow, leaned his lithe, athletic body forward, and in a succession of heaves and pulls, dragged it far up on the sand. His flashlight showed him, in the bottom of the boat, a white handkerchief and a scrap of paper. Hm! He examined the fairy-like bit of linen, with a neat, hand-embroidered monogram in one corner. He felt a queer sensation about his heart that said, "Possession. It is mine. Hers, but *mine*."

The bit of paper had been trampled upon and was slightly soiled. He picked it up, crumpled it, and tossed it toward the lake.

Then, with a sense of duty well done, he directed his steps toward the loggia gate, and to bed. In a little while, the wind would come, whip the lake into a white-capped fury, against whose waves no little boat could make the slightest progress. And until that storm should subside, he could not go to her, nor she to him, except they take a long, roundabout way. But he would do that; he would not let tomorrow pass without seeing her. His excuse could be to return the handkerchief.

7.

BERYL stood on the veranda of her tiny cottage, listening to his footsteps receding down the board walk, toward his dinghy. A little later, he was moving out across the black lake, with only the light of his flashlight visible, like a fallen star moving . . .

He *was* that. He was Jim Grabill as she had once believed him to be before she had seen him as he was — before also, she had had the eyes of her own understanding opened. Jim Grabill had died, and from his grave had risen his identical twin, Timothy — it was so in her own heart . . .

The thought illustrated the Bible doctrine of dying to self, she thought, and being raised again in newness of life. The old self was dead; the new only, was alive. She would weave that truth into her story tomorrow morning. It was in the will of God surely, that she had come here — even to this identical spot in His universe, that she might be the channel of this great truth to others . . .

Dead to Jim; alive to Tim: How very *very much* alive! So much so that she could not believe it was true, and therefore believed it all the more. Yet things were moving too swiftly. And there were too many things to separate them. The codicil, for instance —

She had taken it with her on the trip across, thinking perhaps that she ought to confide in Tim, tell him the exact truth before he found out in some way that might make him misunderstand. She had expected the old man to drive over in the afternoon, but he had forgotten. Tim had said he was getting to be very forgetful since Elizabeth's death. And he was old, and childish, and might be considered incapable of knowing his own mind; in which case, according to Martini, who was the law personified, the codicil would be invalid . . .

58

The doctors could be wrong. Old John may have had some premonition of soon-coming death, which was superior knowledge to that of men who dealt only with known physical laws. Old John was a faithful Christian, who had lived intimately with his God, and it may have been made known to him in some way.

The little light out on the lake faded until she could see it no more. Things were in a pretty tangle, she thought, and kept on thinking, trying to see her way through.

And while she stood, and thought, the clouds that were moving ahead of the storm came and covered the sky, hiding the stars. In a little while the rain came, gently at first, like the soft whispers of worshippers in the old church back home, before the first solemn notes of the organ hushed them all into silence. Rain on the roof! In little-girlhood days, there had been cozy afternoons when she and Dora Jeanne, four years younger than she, had played the game of dolls in the upstairs of the old home. It was Dora Jeanne who had always opened the attic door so they could hear the rain . . .

"Hear the rain, Dolly?" Dora Jeanne, with her brown curls tossing with the spirited toss of her head, would stand in the open attic doorway, and look unafraid into the dark and always mysterious attic, and say: "The fairies are dancing on the roof . . ." And then, her very blue eyes distant with mystery, Dora Jeanne would launch into a colorful story of the brave prince who some day would come riding on his snow-white horse to carry her away. Always in her stories Dora Jeanne was the princess. . . . And always the charger was white. . . . *Like a white boat!*

Sometimes, too, on rainy days, there had been violent electric storms, and the game of dolls would collapse, and the two would cling to each other in fear, and cringe with each new crash of thunder. And if it were night, they would hide their faces from the lightning. . . . Dear little Dora Jeanne. She was a young woman now, and still waiting and dreaming for her prince to come. She could not adjust herself to the commonplace; had not learned that roses must have thorns, that success comes only after toilsome apprenticeship ...

Low thunder rumbles gave place suddenly to one terrific crash, simultaneous with a blinding light that fell like a white-hot ball from the sky. In that blinding flash of light Beryl saw the great elm in front of the cottage split wide open. And in another flash, which illumined all the sky and the tossing lake, she saw a jagged white scar that ran the length of the elm from the first great limb to the ground, saw that limb dangling against the trunk like a paralyzed arm against a strong man's body. Death could come as quick as that — to a tree, or to a man. To anybody any time. It was wise to be ready, — to have one's heart made clean through faith in Him whose blood was shed voluntarily for the remission of sins.

The thought flashed into her mind instantaneously with the first crash of the storm: *To a tree, or to a man ...!*

She thrust her hand into her topper pocket for the folded piece of paper. But it was not there.

And while the storm raged outside, she searched for the paper — on the porch, inside the cottage, in her topper pockets, everywhere, and did not find it.

Perhaps, in the boat, when she had — almost fallen. It might be lying on the beach, or on the dock out there, or in the water, where now, great waves were rolling in, crashing against her rowboat

And then, alarmingly, came the thought — It might have fallen in Tim's dinghy, and he would find it. Perhaps he had already found it!

Suddenly it seemed a tragic thing if he should, without her having told him first. Why had she let the whole day pass by without showing it to him! But then, the old man had asked her not to.

She could not recall when she had ever been hysterical, or when she had not been able to control her feelings. For to be a business woman, she had had to school herself to remain calm, poised in all emergencies — not like emotional women on radio skits, who went to pieces on the least provocation, and sobbed hysterically, while writer-created heroes consoled and soothed them back to normalcy. . . . It was unfair to womanhood to give such stories to the public. Ten million women, listening every day to sobbing heroines! Such distortions, dramatized, might establish in the minds of those ten million the notion that such was the norm of womanhood . . .

In the story Beryl would write, the heroine would be strong, poised in emergencies: in storms, under great mental strain. . . . Once when she had been a little girl, lightning had struck a giant maple in their pasture; and six horses, standing there, sheltering themselves from the rain, had dropped like as many logs, and lay sprawled across each other in a death heap. After the storm she and Dora Jeanne, wading barefoot in the new puddles, had come suddenly upon the horrifying scene, and Dora Jeanne's lips had quivered, and she had stamped her little foot in rebellion and said, "I don't like God for doing that! If He was going to do it, whyn't He let the *white* horse live anyway . . . !" The horse's name had been *Jim!*

And Beryl, in the presence of death, had been afraid. But she would not be afraid now. Not with the Gradys next door, and with the peace of God that passeth understanding in her heart. She was a business girl, with controlled nerves. That was why dynamic, bragadoccio Martini had been satisfied with her work, had preferred her to all other stenographers in his office.

She *would* not lose control of herself now! Even if the will were lost — even if Timothy Grabill might find it — *had* found it . . .

Rain on the roof now was like hail. Lightning played grimly, fiercely across the sky, while thunder crashed simultaneously with each terrific flash. . . . She stood clinging to the doorknob, pressing herself against the jamb, and always, with every new lighting up of the world, she saw the twisting scar on the face of the elm, and seeing it, thought of how quickly a thing like that could happen . . . *To anybody any time!*

Sobbing, hysterical women . . . ! She pitied those writer-made weaklings. She would hate herself if she went to pieces now, and yet, *How can I help it! If I don't find the will . . . !*

Suddenly she was out in the storm with her flashlight, running here, there, down the slippery board walk, falling, rising, slipping off into the sand which filled her oxfords. The rain went through her topper as if it had been a sieve, and soaked her to the skin. She pitied weaklings, hated them almost . . .

At the dock, where the waves crashed in, she shot her beam of light all along the shore, examined every breaking whitecap, every white shell. She saw a bit of white riding a wave, saw it come seething in, and go back again. *"I must find it! If I don't, then I know I dropped it in his boat, and he'll find it! He has found it, — unless I do!*

She flung herself into the lake after the receding bit of white that had washed in. In the angry water, she stumbled and fell against the side of her heaving boat. She might have dropped it in her own boat, she thought. Then she lost her balance and slipped sidewise over the edge of the gunwale. The flashlight fell into the water, lay on the sandy bottom, making the water there look like a phosphorescence of the sea . . .

The storm roared on. Lightning, thunder, rain in great wave-sheets. In the cottage next door, the Gradys were awake. Grady himself tossed on his raincoat, and with his powerful electric lantern, went out. He saw the white scar on the elm. All lights were out in the cabins, and it would be his duty to call at each one and reassure the campers, to help them light kerosene lamps if necessary.

His light beam darted here and there, out across the heaving lake, the docks. Above the roar of the wind, he thought he heard a call for help, coming from the lake. Of course it could not be — yet it had been a woman's voice. But not from the lake surely. He knocked at the door of Beryl's cabin, called loudly. His sonorous voice was lost in the roar of the wind and there was no answer. The scar on the elm! Had anything happened to the brave little lady who had been sent to them by Mrs. Schaeffer? — "Take good care of her, and keep an eye out for her at all times. She's a precious girl . . ."

He pushed himself into the cottage, swung the light here, there, called again, "Miss Lane! Are you here? Are you all right?"

The cottage was empty. Was she out in the storm, perhaps? He lumbered through the house, and out into the swirling night. He had seen her boat come in a half hour ago — an hour ago, with her escort. He had seen them coming up the walk together, seen him drive back across the lake.

He followed the long white light of his lantern down to the dock, half running, pushing against the wind.

And there he found her, and carried her back up the walk to the caretaker's headquarters. Mrs. Grady threw open the door and let them in, closing it quickly after them to shut out the storm.

It was a strange emotion — that of being carried in a strong man's arms, with the rain beating hard against her face, thunder crashing and crashing like giant trees falling in a forest. For a moment she thought she heard a hysterical heroine on a radio skit, crying and gasping for breath, only there was no deep-voiced lover to console her. There was a deep voice but it was Sam Grady's, and he was saying, "Here she is, Molly! Alive and well."

Had she fainted? she wondered. Things in the lamp-shadowed room swung dizzily for a moment, steadied themselves, and she looked up into the face of Mrs. Grady, who, for a moment, was not Mrs. Grady, but her own mother, tired and haggard with overwork and the cares of the home.

"I — I lost it, Mother, and the storm killed him. It happened before I could —"

————

Beryl, lying on the studio couch in the Gradys' front room, tossed off the feeling of hysteria, drank the cup of tea which Mrs. Grady brought. Sam had gone out again to make the rounds of the cottages. The storm was still at its highest fury, but she was safe now.

When Sam came back, his orders were, "You're staying under our roof to-night! Think we want to trust anybody to stay alone who doesn't know enough to come in out of the rain? What would Mrs. Schaeffer think of us — letting you play around in a storm like that!" His voice was jestingly gruff.

"I was trying to get my flashlight, — Did you find it? It was in the lake there by the boat."

"Flashlight!" The gorilla looked across at his wife, and said, "She keeps her flashlight on the bottom of the lake!"

She liked the Gradys. They were such unpretentious people. They too, were drinking of the cup of cold water, from the hand of Mrs. Schaeffer. She recalled that he had been struggling along on a government relief roll when Mrs. Schaeffer had found him. They had been very gracious to her during her brief stay here, — Mrs. Grady, a chirping, motherly soul; and he, always mockingly gruff, with feelings that were the opposite of his surly words.

It was near midnight before the storm moved on, and they could get to sleep. It was good, Beryl thought, as she settled herself in cozy blankets on the studio couch in the Grady cottage, so good to have friends, and to be a part of a great world-wide program, planned and supervised by a Risen Lord, being watched over and cared for by Him.

In the adjoining room, she heard the deep, low voice of Grady say to his wife, "Just like God pulling me out of my troubles, I picked up that little thing and carried her in out of the storm."

She heard a comfortable sigh from Mrs. Grady, and unintelligible words. A little later, their lamp went out, and Beryl lay in the dark thinking, and admitting to herself that she too, could go to pieces. Her nerves still trembled, and she knew that the experiences of the night would never be forgotten.

She could hear the lake, still heaving after the storm, and she thought that her own emotions were like that, and knew it would take time before she would be herself again. Tomorrow, she must dig deep into her story plot, and write and write and write. She must not allow the things of her own life to impress her more deeply than those of her story. She must write, *without interruption*. Not even Timothy Grabill with his mysterious gray eyes, his gentle manner and bearing, must interfere, either in person, or by storming into her thoughts and carrying her away . . . He was coming tomorrow, in midafternoon, and they were motoring to a little island, to explore, to take pictures, climb rocky cliffs . . .

Her thoughts flung themselves away on a tangent, moved in an ethereal world; and in that world she was writing and writing, making wills, and losing them, making words, stealing words, stealing his words . . . *stealing his love* . . .

8.

I T WAS a new day. There was a new lake, calm and clean, a new sky, a washed world. Only the great white scar on the elm, and the dangling limb, indicated that last night nature had been on a rampage.

For awhile, before settling herself at the typewriter, Beryl went down to the dock. Grady had pulled her boat far up on the sand and turned it bottom side up. Yonder, across the blue water, was the old man's dinghy, like a long white rock in the sun. Beyond the row of new birch, the Nest glistened like white marble, the sun porch on the roof was like a lookout on an ocean liner . . . This afternoon they would ride away in old John's dinghy.

The sun smiled back at her; the gulls over the lake circled low, tossed themselves here and there in careless rhythm. The little book in Beryl's hand, opened to a favorite series of verses, said, *"If a man love Me . . . I will manifest myself unto him . . . and my Father, will love him, and we will come to him and make our abode with him."*

She must give the abiding Guest — Father, Son and Holy Spirit — the key to every room within her heart . . . Last night's strange fear, her wild terror, and her frantic search for the codicil, seemed this morning, like a weird dream that had happened to somebody else. Uncle John would be driving over some time to-day, and she would explain to him that the codicil was lost. There were some changes he wished to make, so the loss of the original would not matter. The only thing was, if Timothy should find it!

"Be anxious for nothing" the little book in her hand said, and the divine Medium for the revelation of spiritual realities, annihilated distance, and made the Lord Jesus — the one whose Name was Jesus, — a conscious Presence. *O Christ, Thou*

*art equal to any emergency! And if I am in Thy will, I AM
triumphant!*

In what way, she wondered, would the old man wish to
change the codicil? For a moment, she wondered what might
happen if Jim should come and find it.

A careful search up and down the beach, and along the
board walk, and especially near the dock where last night she
had for a bewildered and beautiful moment been upheld by
Tim's strong arms — No, there was no use to look for it here.
It was lost in the lake, probably, and would never be found.

She went back to her cottage and was soon walking among
the stars of her story. Her heroine, in white, stood once more
at the urn-shaped bird-bath on the flowered lawn. At the beach,
a young man in blue slacks moved about, singing at his
work . . .

At nine, Mrs. Grady came with lunch, steaming coffee, fried
cakes with bacon. That had been the arrangement from the
beginning: Lunch was to be brought at nine each morning,
so that the time required for preparing it, would be spared
Beryl. After that there were to be no interruptions, not even
for the mail; for letters had a way of breaking into her story,
that made it difficult to find the thread again. She would go
for the mail herself, when the right time came.

Lunch over, Beryl settled down again to her typewriter . . .
"The leaden sky came suddenly alive; jagged three-bladed
lightnings split the heavens, thunder crashed, rolled in earth-
shaking vibrations from sky to sky . . ." Never had she had
more freedom in writing; and while she wrote she seemed to
see her book complete, bound and jacketed, and going into all
the world to preach the gospel.

The shaft of sunlight coming in through the cottage window, crept around slowly until it shone in directly from the
south.

At three, Timothy was coming for her.

At two, she had had her afternoon siesta, and was ready. She
was lying on her porch hammock reading, when she heard the

motor, put-putting across the lake. She waited until she heard it stopping at the dock, then she arose and went to the screen door to watch him, and saw, not Timothy, but Uncle John. She opened the door and went down the walk to meet him.

"Good afternoon, Miss Lane," he greeted her wheezily. He gazed up at her fondly, and she thought for a moment there was a troubled look in his eyes.

"Tim took me in to Dr. Mahone this morning and he fixed me up. Said it wasn't my heart altogether. See here —" He pushed up the sleeve of his khaki shirt and displayed a pink, oblong spot above the elbow. "Doc took a sample of blood out of my ear, and tested it and said it didn't have enough oxygen carrying content. Anemia, he called it, and so he gave me a shot of liver and iron. He's getting some capsules of the same thing from the city today and I'll add them to my walleye pike diet. A week from now I'll have so much pep I'll probably want to throw my motor away and use oars — I feel a hundred percent better already although doctor says absolutely no rowing for awhile. Had a hard time convincing Timothy that I should drive over alone . . ."

He shuffled across the sand to the edge of the dock, clambered to a standing position beside her.

She was thinking what an adorable old gentleman he was, his grizzled neatly trimmed mustache and goatee making him look almost distinguished. There was gentleness in his expressive blue-gray eyes. He might seem a bit odd to those who would not understand, but what old man ever lived who did not develop some distinguishing characteristic — a mail-order diet; a hobby of some sort or other? And they were all forgetful —

"See what I did last night, in the middle of the night, when the storm was making so much noise, and God was shaking His world so hard with His thunder?" He held out to her an angular left hand that trembled as he poised it in a horizontal position. On the middle finger was tied a piece of red string.

"I did that so I wouldn't forget again. And just as soon as Timothy would let me, I motored over. Doc told me not to worry about my heart any more so I'm not. Uh — you haven't told anybody, have you? About the codicil, I mean? I suppose Timothy really ought to know, but he wouldn't agree with it at all.

"You see, I had everything willed to Elizabeth —" A sob squeezed off the old man's voice and there was a painful moment before he could continue. He stood, blinking his eyes, looking out across the blue lake toward the Nest. Then he lifted his silver-topped cane and pointed to a lone gull dipping in the wind. "I never see one of them without thinking how white her life was; and the wings make me think of angels, and the angels remind me of Lazarus being carried by angels into Abraham's Bosom —"

He broke off suddenly. "What was I saying? There was something I wanted to tell you." He frowned. "It's very confusing, being an old man, and being so forgetful. Hm! — What —?"

"Was it about — Elizabeth, perhaps?"

He seemed to remember. "All stories don't have happy endings, do they? And some that do end happily, are tragedies later on. Do you know —?" His eyes were following the dip and toss of the gull as it circled, dropped, zoomed up again, continued its zigzagging course, *alone*.

In the silence they both watched, until from across the lake, unannounced, came other gulls, dozens of them, and Beryl thought: "And suddenly there was with the angel, a multitude of the heavenly host, praising God and saying, 'Glory to God in the highest, and on earth, Peace . . . 'Peace' . . .'"

Uncle John Bishop sighed wearily, and did not finish his sentence.

"You're tired," Beryl said to him. "Come and sit on my veranda awhile and watch the lake. I'll make you a cup of tea." With that, she remembered the fish-fry at the Spragues last night, the moment with Tim on the dock here — and all the rest of the strange night.

He followed her up the walk. "Maybe I *am* a bit tired," he puffed. "The storm kept me awake. I thought for awhile I was going to have another spell."

"But you didn't."

"No. But I got up and dressed and Tim and I talked in front of the fire. We thought about you over here, and I remembered my promise."

They were sitting at a little table now, in a corner of the veranda.

He saw, then, the great white scar on the elm, and the limb dangling. "That happen last night?" He pointed with his cane.

She nodded. He focused his eyes on the top of the scar. "Makes me think of something I read this morning, which maybe you can use in your book. The very minute the Lord Jesus died on the cross out on Golgotha's hill, away down town in Jerusalem, in the temple, the great veil that separated the holy place from the holy of holies, was rent in twain from top to bottom, signifying, according to later revelation, that there was nothing now to bar a man's entrance into the heart of God except, of course, his sin; that Jesus, Himself, *was* the veil; and when his flesh was torn for us, it gave us a new Way to God. In fact that's what it says, —"

She was busy at the little gas stove, making tea. When she came back, he said, "It says, 'Having therefore, brethren, boldness to enter into the holiest by the blood of Jesus, by a new and living way, which he hath consecrated for us, through the veil, that is to say, His flesh . . .' That's in Hebrews ten —" He lifted a trembling cup to his lips. His eyes were on the place where the lightning had struck, and his thoughts, she supposed, were looking beyond the veil to his Elizabeth, who was on the other side. A little later, he saw the red string on his finger, and said, "And now if you will bring the codicil, we'll make the changes and get it off to my lawyer. It's the way things are going in the world that has decided me —." He was looking at the scar on the elm again. He leaned forward, the cup of tea still in his hand.

"There's a storm going to break all over the world before long. The thunderheads are gathering now. Everything will look like the most terrible chaos. And it *will* be for millions of people. Last night I read something by Harrison, though — maybe you can use it in your book. I wrote it down — somewhere." He was shuffling his hands in and out of pockets.

"Here it is — 'The redeemed soul, living in fellowship with Christ, is one spot on earth where there is no chaos.' Isn't that beautiful? Do you think maybe you can use it?"

She knew she could. The dear old saint! Even if he should live only a little while, the fragrance of his life would live on in her book.

She must bring his thoughts back to the matter in hand now. She must tell him that the codicil had been lost, perhaps in the lake, and that they would have to make an entirely new one.

"I feel foolish writing my own name into a will," she began. "Hadn't you better have your lawyer come. It will look to everyone who knows about it, that I used undue influence."

He set his tea cup into its saucer, looked at her startled. "Hm! It would, wouldn't it? I never thought of that." He stroked his goatee pensively. Then his little blue eyes lit up and he said, "I tell you what I'll do, I'll have Timothy draw five thousand dollars for you. You could probably use it right away anyhow. And now that it looks like I'm going to live a long time — Say, that's the best yet!" He was as enthusiastic as a schoolboy.

And then, without warning, Beryl saw Sam Grady coming up the path with — was it? — It *was* JIM Grabill, laughing, talking animatedly.

"It's — *Jim!*" she exclaimed in low tones to the old man, and immediately she was standing.

The old man stood also, peering at the visitors through his upper lenses.

"Company for you," Grady announced. "Good afternoon, Mr. Bishop," he said, nodding to the old man. "And now if you'll excuse me, there's a boat coming in down at the lodge, and I'll have a string of fish to put on ice . . ." Grady turned in his slow easy manner and moved in long strides up the path toward the central lodge.

"Uncle *John!*" Jim Grabill exclaimed. "What are you doing *here!*"

The old man came alive with a suddenness that was startling. Beryl noticed for a fleeting second, the same expression of fear that had been on his face yesterday morning, as he said in a voice higher-pitched than usual, "So you've come back again! Miss — Lane, this is my other nephew, James, the one I — whose name —" Confusion closed the old man's lips.

"We've met before," James said, and Beryl, hearing him say it, remembered with a rush of troubled thoughts, her many experiences with Jim during the past months. This was the other twin, the one to whom she had died, and from whom Timothy Grabill had come to set her free. An old love was dead, and a new one was arising like a sun, to lighten all her life — only it was not yet love-fully-formed, but only in the making; it was little farther in its growth than the purest of respect, the chief corner-stone of a love that would last.

Uncle John looked about nervously, studied the dial of a heavy-chained gold watch, caught his breath, while his forehead crinkled into a worried pucker. "It's time I should fly back to my nest." To Jim he said, "I suppose you'll be coming over. Your brother is here, and —" Again John Sylvester Bishop frowned, as if trying to remember something that was disturbing him, yet was elusive. There was also, very definitely noticeable, Beryl thought, a dislike in his eyes for James Grabill. There was also fear.

Beryl thought she understood the cause of that fear, when a second later Jim said, "How's your heart behaving, Uncle John? Acting up any this past week? I've been worried about you. That's why I came back to-day —" To Beryl, he explained, "He's been having heart attacks this summer, and we've been worried."

Uncle John's blue eyes narrowed. "My heart is all right," he said, spiritedly. "I've had a doctor, and he says I'm good for years yet, so you can stop worrying." He turned to go, pushed open the screen door and hobbled out. He did not stop to look back, but hurried down the dock to his dinghy.

He had come, and he had gone. She stood beside Jim, watching, trying to decide what to do, then, impulsively, she thrust open the screen door and ran down the walk after him, calling out to him to wait. She reached the end of the dock at the very moment he was coiling the starter rope around the disc.

She could not let him go without telling him the codicil they had made yesterday was lost . . .

"The codicil —" she began, but he was not listening. He was staring up at her and above her into the sky. Turning, Beryl saw a white gull circling.

Startled, she looked again at the face of the mystical old man who even now seemed to be within the veil. He was in the Presence of God now because the Presence of God was within him.

She began again, — "The codicil —." She told him the whole story, while he listened, a bit absent-mindedly, she thought. He was still watching the gull. Then he gave his attention to the motor, his hand on the knot of the starter cord. "You're like Elizabeth," he said, "one hundred percent honest. But we won't worry about that. I'll make a new one some day next week. I'll have my lawyer come over. Now that I'm going to live, there isn't any need to hurry." He smiled up at her. "I promised Tim I'd be back by three, so —"

She saw his arm move in a swift, sharp pull of the starter cord, heard the immediate roaring response of the motor, and he was off. He did not look back but opened wide the throttle and steered at top speed straight for the pier in front of the Nest.

Beryl stood watching until he was half way across the bay, then because there was nothing else she could do, she turned and walked slowly up the board walk to where Jim was waiting for her — the man who had gone out of her life forever, yet had to-day come back like a demon dispossessed, to torment her.

9

A T THE veranda steps Beryl stopped. On the other side of the new screen she saw both Jim and Tim, both the playboy and the college professor, the man of the world and the fruit-bearing Christian — saw them both in this man whose physical features were in every respect identical to his twin. The past had arisen to do battle with the present, and the battleground was to be her own heart.

Battle? She knew who would be the victor, for he was that already. It would not be easy however, for the vanquished one to acknowledge defeat. The victory at Calvary was like that: There, the God-man had conquered Satan, the prince of this world, yet it remained for the followers of the God-man to *claim* the conquered territory in His Name, before it should become their possession; and even then, the defeated enemy challenged every inch of the victory ground. . . . In her book she would interweave this truth tomorrow . . .

He held open the door for her, stepped back courteously. He could be gallant.

She brought him a cup of tea, and they sat opposite each other at the porch table. Experiences like this were the type which bewildered radio heroines, which swept them along into a mental state that at the proper climax of the skit, collapsed. Her hand trembled as she lifted her cup. . . *The cup!* She would be kind to Jim. She hoped he would not be emotional.

He drew her special delivery letter from his pocket, laid it on the orange blossom design on the oil cloth. For a long time, it seemed, he looked at it with narrowed eyelids. She felt the tenseness of the atmosphere. He was going to be emotional. Or was it her own emotions that were about to open wide the throttle, and go racing with her into the wind, carrying her away from Jim and all that he stood for, all that he wanted her to be and do — which, judged in the light of the Light of the world, were nothing . . .

He set his blue cup in its saucer. "Your letter," he said, "was an invitation to me to come. You know you can't dismiss a man like that so easily."

"How did you know where to find me?"

"Martini's new secretary had just addressed a letter to you, and since I was in the office at that moment for the very purpose of finding out where you were, it was a simple matter. You were wise in coming here, Beryl, for we shall be near each other. My Uncle John who was here a minute ago, owns a beautiful estate over there, and I sometimes spend a week or two with him in the summer —"

She was unaware of having interrupted him until afterward, when she asked, "Why didn't you tell me you have a twin brother?"

He scowled. "You've met him too, I suppose. He's almost as eccentric as Uncle John. We live in different worlds, so I don't bother to tell my friends about him. Has Uncle John made the rounds here with his fish? He is an invaluable nuisance to resorters who don't know how to fish but who like to put on front —"

"Timothy seems to be very intelligent," she said. It gave her a feeling of triumph to use his first name, to let Jim know that she knew him that well.

Jim's brows arched. "Intelligent?"

"And wise. '*The fear of the Lord is the beginning of wisdom,*' you know."

"I don't know that. I would challenge that statement, at least as far as Tim is concerned. In any event, I came to talk to you about *you* — and us. You couldn't have selected a hide-away more suited to circumstances. In fact, I had been planning a little surprise for you. I had Martini inveigled into letting you off for a week — with salary, of course, and at my expense — and we were going to run down here and spend a gay holiday in the Nest, — that's the name of my estate over there. That is, it's not mine yet, but Uncle John has willed it to me, and just as soon as his — when he dies, you and I will be wealthy beyond belief. There are one hundred acres of lake front property adjoining the Nest, and that's included in the will. It's here in the heart of the most popular resort region in the country. Millionaires have been trying to buy it for years . . ."

She let him talk on, let him boast, as he was always doing, — and as Timothy did not do; let him exalt himself, as Tim did not do; let him offer his thousands, as Tim did not do. Timothy had made her rich in friendship. He had given back to her a respect for men which Jim had taken away. Tim had talked of the Vine and the branches, and of the inflow of Life . . .

"As Mrs. James Conwell Grabill, you will spend your summers here, and your winters in Florida, or California, or wherever our whims may take us. There'll be polo, golf, dancing on moonlit terraces in Hawaii, gay nights in old Mexico . . ."

"I wonder if you brought a newspaper from the city. I've been neglecting the war news since I came here. It's hard to believe there is a war, when the lake is like — that." Above the dock a white gull circled, dropped like a bullet to the surface, zoomed up again with a bit of something in its beak. Old John was living in the presence of God *now*. In Christ, one could have access to the holy of holies all the time . . . *"Let us come boldly to the throne of grace . . ."* the Book invited. There was no veil now to bar the entrance to God's heart of love, for the veil was rent in twain —.

"Terrible storm last night," he said, and she looked at the scar on the elm. . . . The wounds of Calvary were the entrance into the holy place — the wounds also by which we might be grafted into the Vine. No wonder St. Paul had said, *"If any man be in Christ, he is a NEW creation . . ."* Before the ingrafting experience, before one began to be a partaker of His Nature, there was only death. For each one there must be a definite time of being grafted in. That experience Jim had never had; and he would never have it until he was willing to surrender his — *death,* and yield to *Life* . . .

"Wind almost blew me off the road," he said, lifting his blue cup, while she saw the flash of a diamond on his finger. *Diamond* . . . ! There were other uses for diamonds . . .

"But I kept on driving, all night. I stopped at a barber shop in town, and here I am, — and you are treating me like so much dirt."

He had driven all night because of *her?* Or because he did not wish to *lose* her? There was a difference.

Suddenly he reached across the table and seized both her hands. She felt the fierceness of his intensity, while the very dynamic of his personality demanded that she raise her eyes to meet his.

NO, she told herself, she *would* not. A second later she had acceded to his wish, and was hearing him say, while his hands, clinging to hers, trembled: "Beryl, when your letter came, I knew that I had never loved, never would love another woman. I have come not only to tell you but to try to prove it to you."

She struggled to free her hands. She had been brought up on a farm; she had muscles. . . . *Would* she have fallen last night if Timothy had not caught her . . . ?

"Those hands were not made for work, Beryl," Jim was saying. "They were made for love. They're perfect, like you are — except for your determination to want a career."

She stood. He stood. She was glad the table was between them, even though she knew he would not take her in his arms without her consent.

She twisted her hands free, lifted the tea cups, one in each hand, carried them inside to the sink in the kitchenette. When she came back he was standing at the door, smoking. From across the lake, driving at full speed, came old John's dinghy, the motor roaring like an airplane motor, and in the stern, his hair unruly in the wind, was Timothy. He raised a bare brown arm in salute, and Beryl, in a flash, was out on the board walk, running down to the dock to meet him — a streak of color; goldenrod hair tucked into blue snood, blue and white oxfords striking the boards gaily, like a child running to meet a playmate. Tim was that to her, as well as friend and lover. No, he was not yet the latter but he would become so. She knew it after last night — more so than ever, now that she had seen Jim again.

Tim shut off the motor, tilted it in a quick, forward pull to keep the propeller off the sand of the bottom. The dinghy glided swiftly toward the beach, scraped hard against the sand, stopped.

There was a smile on Timothy Grabill's face. "Am I on time?" he asked, looking at his wrist-watch. "I was afraid Uncle John would forget to come back, but he was right on the dot for a change."

In the boat was a small camp stove, beside it a basket covered with a linen tablecloth, neatly folded.

"Geneveve fixed the lunch — most of it — we'll do the rest when we get there. She threatened all kinds of corrective punishment if I didn't take good care of you. She fell in love with you last night — she and Hartford. You should hear Hartford talk. Are you ready?" He was standing now, extending his hand to assist her into the dinghy.

Was it right to leave Jim this way? She was ready, all except for her topper. It might be cool later in the day.

"One minute," she said, and ran back up the board walk.

"No apologies." Jim intercepted any explanation she might have made. "Run along and have a good time. I'm used to having him break into my affairs."

"We'd planned this last night. I didn't know you were coming —!" She stopped short. What need had she to apologize to Jim!

"I'll stay here on the porch until you're out of sight," he said. "Don't tell him I'm here. It might put a crimp in his fun. But I warn you, Beryl. All is not gold that glitters. Remember I told you."

Her cheeks flushed crimson. Bitterly she resented what he had said. Bewildered, she went inside for her topper, came out, and went hurrying down the walk toward the dinghy, free as a bird released from its cage, yet feeling as if somehow her wings had been clipped by the words he had said.

"Ready!" Beryl exclaimed cheerily to Timothy when she reached the dock. She gave him her hand and let him steer her to her accustomed seat facing the stern.

Timothy, all eyes for Beryl, solicitous that she be comfortably seated, was unaware of the man standing in the shadow of the shattered old elm, just inside the screened porch door. He shoved the boat out into deep water, leaping onto the gunwale as it left the sands, balanced his way past the girl in the multi-colored jumper dress, sat down in the stern. A brief interval later, after he had turned the dinghy about with an oar, the motor leaped into roaring life, and they were off.

The man in the shadow of the elm stood watching until the boat was like a white gull riding the surface of the water. Then he came out onto the board walk, the screen door slamming carelessly behind him. He tossed a cigarette stub onto the sands, strolled toward the dock, then stopped abruptly, clenched his fists and muttered, "Some day he'll cross my path once too often!"

10.

THE man in the blue slack suit, and the girl in the multi-colored jumper dress, were on their way to explore an island — and, as he had planned, each other's minds. Incidentally also, and fundamentally, he was thinking at this very moment, while the dinghy roared out across the lake toward the Nest, he wanted to do a bit of exploration in a newly-discovered island in his own mind.

Last night, in the sun room atop the Nest, which was always his sleeping room when he visited Uncle John, he had admitted to himself that that island was indeed an enchanted island. The emotions that had come to him in that moment when he was holding her in his arms — very awkwardly, he had decided afterward — were those for which he had long waited and which he knew he must experience before he allowed himself to think seriously of any woman.

Think seriously! Could this be rightly called *thinking?* *Think,* as an intransitive verb, meant to exercise the mind *actively;* last night, with the rain pounding on the roof, and pelting against the glass windows of the spacious sun room, while grim lightnings leaped jaggedly across the leaden sky, he had thought only *passively.* Already he was being carried along in a more or less helpless state. This, he compelled himself to think, must not continue. He would fall in love — an expression of which he did not approve at all — in a wholly sensible and philosophical manner. . . . Love was not a reservoir or a crater to fall into, but a new experience — *an island to explore . . .*

Then had come the first terrific crash of the storm, and he had heard old John downstairs stumbling about in the dark, had gone down to keep him company.

Among other things, they had talked about the young woman who lived across the bay, whom Timothy Grabill had met that morning for the first time — who now sat facing him in the dinghy, her very blue eyes not seeing him at all but looking over his shoulder at the receding shore.

Last night, Uncle John, the flickering light from the fireplace making him look like a gaunt old tree that some day soon might weather its last storm, had stood near the open door of the loggia, watching the heaving lake.

At first no words passed between them. Tim waited until he knew that what he should say would be welcomed; for at times like this old John was seemingly only bodily present. His mind was shut away somewhere in a mystical room where he communed with his thoughts, and where the Master dwelt.

Quite suddenly then, Old John Sylvester Bishop had turned, closed the heavy oak door and walked back to his great chair near the fire. "Timothy," he began wheezily, and coughed a smothered dry cough. He reached for a book on the radio table beside him.

Timothy stirred up the fire, watched the sparks shower upward, smiled to himself as the new flames licked hungrily at the logs at the very instant of their birth. . . . A moment ago those flames had not been in existence. Life and hunger were closely related. In a fire; in a human being. In physical life; in spiritual. Where there was no hunger in the soul of a man, there had been no new birth.

He waited for the old man to speak. He did not have to wait long. "The young lady, Timothy. You are going to marry her." It was a calm statement of fact.

It came as a shock, a delightful shock; yet Timothy knew that it was true. He would do everything in his power to make it true.

They had talked about many other things there by the fire, and Timothy had stored away wisdom for his new book. At length the storm had passed, and he had gone once more to the sun room, and there, with the blinds raised on the side overlooking the lake, he had watched until the sky cleared itself of clouds, and the stars came out, and the wind died away. He had gone to sleep to the rhythm of waves splashing against the shore.

The storm passed; the night also. And now, under a sky loosely patterned with great cauliflower clouds, with blue as clear as the blue field of an American flag, Timothy Grabill looked across the lake toward the Nest where last night he had done his dreaming, and knew again that Uncle John was right. Knew it without knowing it. For today was to be a day of exploration. He had driven across fifteen minutes ago, anticipating the worst. She would not be at all like she had seemed yesterday and last night. She would be like other women, even in her dress. She would be wearing some dashing thing of flash and color unsuited to the dream girl he had created in his mind . . .

But she had not. And he was disturbingly well pleased.

"There," he said, when the dinghy neared the cottage where the Spragues lived, "one hundred feet out from shore is the place where Elizabeth was drowned."

Drowned! The word came with a terrific shock to Beryl. Old John's lovely Elizabeth! Her hands on the sides of the boat tightened. They were driving over the very spot *now.*

Her eyes sought those of the man whose face wore a strange tenseness. He had throttled the motor until its put-putting was slow and gentle, and the waves against the boat were soft like the whispers of neighbors visiting in a cemetery.

"She loved the lake so. Uncle John loved her with a love such as I'd never before seen in a father. It was almost like worship." He swung the boat toward the cottage, for Geneveve was out on the dock, waving them to come in.

In the light of day, Hartford Sprague's Jenny seemed more than ever a grand little person. "I forgot to put in the olives," she said, waving a bottle like a baton, beating the rhythm of a song that was evidently singing itself in her mind. "Listen!" she exclaimed cheerily, and Beryl thought how much she was like a gay little canary as she trilled:

"He is the Source of my contentment,
He is the fountain of my joy . . ."

When, a little later, the dinghy was swinging around the promontory toward the shore where were the summer homes of the wealthy, Tim said, "Some day we'll be singing that in our churches —" He sang it now himself, with a lilting baritone which she decided she liked very much, as she was liking everything else about him — *"He is the Source —"*

Both the words and the melody were new to her but she felt their power to create in one the spirit of worship, and she sang with him, content. The motor hid from them the full beauty of their harmony, which without being heard, could be felt and enjoyed.

"If you'll excuse me," she said and reached for her notebook which lay on the seat behind her. "I've just thought of something important which will have to be inserted in my last chapter." She dashed off a paragraph in shorthand, which, when deciphered and polished would read:

"The girl in the multi-colored play togs, her right hand trailing in the passing waters, looked languidly out across the lilting waves. White clouds like great heaps of wool, were piled high in the south-eastern sky, and above them were thin veils of cirrus formation, like old cobwebs floating. The shoreline drifted slowly past, gulls tumbled about overhead, their white wings moving in rhythm to the waves. The odor of spray and seaweed hung lightly in the air. The splashing of the water against the prow of the boat was soft and gentle like rain on the roof — with an opened attic door. Her lover had come riding, not upon a white charger, but in a white boat — and with a white heart. . . . She knew she was going to fall desperately in love with the man in the stern of the boat, whose mystic gray eyes were upon her every moment . . ."

Timothy waited until she had stopped writing, then he said jestingly, "I teach Freshman Composition at Phillips. I'm supposed to be an expert along that line. If you'd care to read me what you've written —"

Again as last night, when he had accused her of stealing his love, so now, she blushed tempestuously. He did not finish his sentence, for her crimson cheeks and neck carried him away to his own new island.

And so their afternoon began. It ended after sunset. Coming back, Tim steered along the shore where were the homes of the wealthy, of the very latest in architectural style and design, where long white docks pushed far out into the lake, where were moored high-powered runabouts and sailboats. At the ends of the docks were mail boxes, bearing the names of families of reputation in the social and business world. One name, especially, Beryl noticed, and strained her eyes to see the initials; but already they were too far past, and the shadows from the trees on the shore prevented clear vision. But that name was Martini. Was it her employer, perhaps? Had he a summer home here? Her employer, also the mortgagee who held not only the mortgage on the Lane fruit farm, but its title. For in this state, she knew, a mortgage was "the conveyance of the legal title," and Martini was regarded by the law as "the actual *purchaser* of the land, to the amount of his claim." How like a great northern Martini was, hiding here and there, always waiting for the unwary. Yet he had been kind. He had given Beryl employment in his office. He had also been willing to release her that she might write her book. Did he hope, perhaps, that in the end Martini might profit, in that through the book's success he might receive again the money invested in the mortgage?

Timothy was steering straight across the lake now, at high speed, leaving behind them as they raced along, a turbulent train of pink and rose and gold wavelets which were but the departed sun's own train, mirrored in the water.

It had been a radiant day. They had talked of many things and places and people; they had told each other the stories of their own first spiritual awakenings, and finally she had explained to him the philosophy which was to be the theme of her book — *A Cup of Cold Water*. He knew that from this day on, he would watch each action of his own, especially in the seemingly little and unimportant things, so that no man could say truthfully that he was not manifesting the Christ life of others. . . . Zacchaeus had been won by the Master's doing the *extra* thing, rugged fishermen had been given an extra large netful of fishes, and immediately 'the disciple whom Jesus loved' had recognized Him and said, "It is the Lord!" So, Timothy Grabill would live, and unbelieving men would come to believe, and watching his life, would say, "It is the Lord."

Neither of them spoke during the fast drive across, for they were listening again to the things they had said to each other during the afternoon, and to the Spirit's interpretation of them to their own hearts. Timothy, swayed by this girl's passion to make Christ known through her book, resolved to give the cup of which she had told him, to one who, above all men that he knew, was undeserving: *He would give the cup even to his own brother, Jim* . . .

And Beryl, watching the multi-colored sky over his shoulder, was remembering the things that he had said were being written in his book manuscript, and which, he had confessed, had once lifted him from a dull and unsatisfactory spiritual life, into one of triumph. She was thinking of the true Vine and of the branches, of which she herself was one, united to Him in vital connection, receiving from Him, through the inflow of His Life, both life and victory and the supply of every spiritual need. *He* was the source of her contentment, her joy, her triumph over sin and sins. In this incomparable relationship with the invisible Christ, He was always near. He was *nearer than near.* He was her very life. . . . In giving the cup of cold water, she was but manifesting to others His love, His tenderness, His courtesy. She must permit no unworthy thought or ambition, no cherished sin to block the channel and thus hinder Him from manifesting Himself to her, and through her to others. He had come into the world to give His life *for us;* He lived now to give His life *to us,* and *through* us. Tomorrow early in the morning, she would be at her desk, her flying fingers typing out this new and wonderful thing.

Grady and his Molly were at the dock to greet them when they came gliding in. "Telegram for you, Miss Lane," Grady said, handing her a yellow envelope. "Western Union phoned out from town, and when I discovered it wasn't a death notice, and could wait until you came back — if you ever did — I didn't bother to hunt you up. Of course we didn't expect you to come home so late." Sam turned to Molly, slipped a long arm about her plump waist and said, "Molly and I would have worried if we hadn't known you were safe with Tim. Young man, don't let this happen again!"

And Timothy promised, "I won't. I'll do it on purpose next time."

Beryl tore open the envelope and in the diffused light from the sky, read:

"COMING TO SPEND A WEEK WITH YOU."

The rectangular bit of yellow paper trembled in her hands as she read the name of the sender, which was DORA JEANNE.

11

TIMOTHY found his brother waiting for him in the drive beside the loggia when he arrived at the Nest. It was startling to face him so soon after his resolution of the afternoon; to give the cup, even to him. Worldly Jim, dashing here and there from one thrill to another, like a gambler whose mania was slot machines, — always, Jim was the loser. There had been, for instance, the affair with Bette Lu, the whirlwind blond, heiress of the Rhinestone millions. The elderly Jasper Rhinestone had been an undiscriminating philanthropist, sowing his gifts hither and yon, but managing somehow, to overlook those institutions and causes that were definitely orthodox in their program and standards. And then, one day — one night, when his only daughter, Bette Lu, had come home decidedly under the influence of liquor, old Jasper had threatened drastic things, among them, disinheritance, compulsory church attendance, and putting her into a convent. Finally, he had seen a full page advertisement of Phillips College, telling of its high educational standards, and its emphasis upon Christian doctrine and living.

Bette Lu had come to Phillips, and one day during her first week there, had sat in Professor Timothy Grabill's classroom, her very dark blue eyes glued to his face, a stubborn little chin held high, defiance in every facial expression. He had talked that first morning on causes — "The power or the efficient agent producing any thing or event." He had talked of the power of the living church through the centuries and had attributed that power to *the perpetual Presence of Christ.*

Later there had been an interview, and efficient Jo Ann, in her little room, which was a part of his office suite, had taken down in shorthand every spoken word. That conversation, neatly typed, was now in Bette Lu's own possession.

After that, Bette Lu had broken with Jim, and Jim, blaming his college professor brother, had never forgiven him, as he had not forgiven him other things in the past, hating him always as the world had hated the Master Himself, *without a cause,* unless indeed, Timothy was thinking as he drove his dinghy across the sky-lit bay to the Nest, *unless hatred* be an inborn trait — which indeed it was with all men, for the Source Book of all spiritual knowledge revealed: *"Now the works of the flesh* [old nature] *are manifest, which are these: Adultery, fornication, uncleanness, lasciviousness, idolatry, witchcraft,* HATRED, *variance . . ."*

And if like produces like, then I must watch my own mind, lest his hate multiply itself in me. I have been kind to Jim; I have treated him courteously and have given him all the love possible, but I have not yet gone out of my way to win him to Christ. I have not done MORE *than any other might have done. I have not done the "extra" thing, nor walked the extra mile. I have given him only luke-warm water."*

The dinghy came gliding up to the dock, where Hartford Sprague stood silhouetted against the horizon, still alight with the afterglow.

Hartford was in a serious mood. He caught the anchor rope, swung the boat's prow over to a dock post. He accepted Jenny's lunch basket from Tim's hand and reached for the camp stove. In another moment Tim was on the dock beside him.

"Today," Sprague said, and paused as if for emphasis, "I've had revealed to me a higher conception of the gospel ministry and my relation to it, than ever before. I don't know how I've missed it all these years, but I have. Perhaps the Lord has held up my going to Africa until I have learned it."

They walked up the narrow dock to the boathouse where they stopped. The pale little moon that had been their companion last night when the four of them had sat on the cottage porch was now, in the twilight, only a dull gray shadow, as thin as a saucer.

"I'll tell you about it in the church tomorrow," Sprague said. "I suppose you'll be there. I'll need you to teach one of my classes. I'm not sure yet which one, but it'll probably be the boys' class, ages ten to fourteen.

"And now, if you'll excuse me, I'll be running along. I've a bit of research to do yet tonight. Jenny's been on her ear waiting for you to get home. She's taken more than a fancy to Miss Lane."

Sprague turned, walked in the little footpath that led past the birches, up the hill to the cottage.

"To his Jenny," Tim thought, and felt within himself a loneliness that was like a vacuum and his thoughts were of the lovely girl in the multi-colored frock who, today, had taught him so much and had inadvertently intensified his loneliness until he knew it would never be dissolved until the day when he would find his true love . . .

At the vine-covered pergola he stopped, looked back. The lake in the afterglow was pink and rose and blue and gold — a thousand hues, it seemed, *living* colors, dancing, playing, tumbling over each other — *multi-colored* . . .

In this frame of mind, his thoughts tender because of the sweetness of his love — Oh, he knew it was that! It required no identification to make itself known. It's cause was deep within himself; its explanation, simply a beautiful fact — under this strange spell, he came face to face with his twin, the man who, outwardly, manifested so many of the evil fruits of his own Adamic nature, but which nature in himself, lay in chains, conquered by the Conqueror. He was more than conqueror because he was more than conquered by the Spirit.

The first he was aware of Jim's presence was when the latter cleared his throat. Tim saw him then, sitting under the steering wheel of his car, in the drive.

"That you, Jim?" he asked, and stopped abruptly. His greeting was answered only with a cold silence. Tim felt the tenseness of it. He remembered that Beryl had run away from Jim. He remembered Bette Lu, and Jim's fierce accusation:

"You lied to her! You are to blame for her throwing me over! YOU FOOL! Don't you know old Rhinestone is worth *millions!*"

He had been worth millions. But only in *money! In stocks and bonds!* and was, therefore, *poor and miserable and blind and naked.*

The car door opened ominously. Jim's movements were quick, angry, yet there was a slowness between movements that bespoke intense emotion. He was wearing a white shirt and gray slacks, his head was bare. He moved with menacing step toward the loggia gate where Tim stood.

His voice trembled. "I suppose, Tim Grabill," he muttered between closed teeth, "you know why I'm here! *Professor* Timothy Grabill, Ph.D.! Cheat! Liar! Thief!"

Tim felt the hot blood leap in his veins. There had been fights in their boyhood days, in which Timothy had been the victor more often than Jim. There had been times, when Tim had, as a boy, looked down into the livid face of his twin whom he had pinioned to the ground by his own muscles, and had not dared to give Jim a moment's freedom, lest he do him bodily hurt. In later years, their warfare had been in the realm of the mind and spirit.

Tonight, Tim knew that Jim was in a mood to do physical violence.

Jim's words hissed, white hot, from between his teeth. *"First,* you rob me of Bette Lu! *That,* I've tried to overlook. But this time you've gone too far. I know now why Beryl has thrown me over! It's you again! It's always you, it has always *been* you, all my life. You've crossed me! —"

Timothy set down the camp stove on the steps, his body went rigid. He knew he could grapple with this brother-adversary, and with muscles kept strong in the gymnasium, hurl his dissipated body to the ground. Could lift and carry him up the hill to the embankment in front of the cottage and hurtle him down upon the rocks. The *Jim* within him challenged him to do it now. *Demanded* that he do it!

But there was Another within, also. He remembered the girl, and her sweet passion to win the lost. His voice trembled when he answered, "I have tried to stop you only from doing wrong, Jim. I—"

"You have butted into my business!"

"I have only been about the Father's business. I'm trying to be my brother's keeper. Do you remember the first brothers?"

"I remember Abel was such a meddling fool that Cain had to kill him! O, *you,* with your religion! You make me sick!"

"By faith, Abel brought a more excellent sacrifice —"

"STOP! I won't listen to it! Do you hear me? It's stuff like that that makes me see red! I don't blame Cain —" Jim turned, rushed to the car, opened and slammed the door violently, rushed back to the loggia gate, kicked viciously at it, dashed again to the car, got in, and sat slumped under the steering wheel, a picture of dejection. He was suffering, Tim knew, more because of the poison his own anger had released in his mind, than for any other reason. He had seen him in tantrums like this before, and now, because he was his brother, he pitied him with a pity that was also love. His own anger was dissolved, and he yearned to go and sit beside his brother, put his arm around him, and tell him of the Saviour's love. He had never done that, he realized now, not in the way it should have been done; not in the spirit of giving the cup of *cold* water.

For a long time, it seemed, Tim stood by the loggia gate, while he listened to the washing of the waves against the shore and the dock, and against old John's dinghy which he and Sprague had beached there, listened also to his brother's heavy breathing, whose temper, after its storm, still heaved within him.

Slowly, then, Tim walked over to the car. Within him, the Spirit cried, "Speak! Give the cup!" Yet he knew Jim would not listen. He would have to demonstrate the gospel by love, and if love would not win him, nothing else would.

Suddenly Jim straightened up. Tim could hear the noise of the friction his hands made as they gripped the steering-wheel.

Jim's voice was a low growl as he said, "We're brothers, Tim, and your Bible says whosoever hateth his brother, is a murderer. I accept the indictment. I *hate* you. And if you want to know how much, keep on meddling in my affairs!"

"Do you wish to know *why* Bette Lu turned you down?"

"I *know* why."

"She surrendered her life to Christ, and—"

"STOP it! I wouldn't believe anything you say!" Viciously Jim stepped on the starter. The motor caught fire, and a moment later the car swung out of the drive and went racing down the forest trail toward the highway.

Tim stood watching until the tail lights disappeared, then he turned and went up to his sunroom to write a letter to Bette Lu, to ask her to write to Jim personally — if she might be so led of the Spirit.

12

THE letter to Bette Lu finished, Timothy went back downstairs to where Uncle John was sitting by the fireplace, reading. He stood for a moment, watching the yellow flames licking lazily at the oak logs.

"I'm driving into town to mail a letter," Tim said. "Anything I can get you — besides the capsules from Dr. Mahone?"

The old man placed his finger on a paragraph, looked up. "Listen to this — the most beautiful thing I've read — I've been reading it over and over. Wish I had known it when I was young; when my mind was clear and before my voice wore out . . ."

The old man took a deep breath, sighed a weary, longing sigh. "If only I were young again —. Tim, you're young and strong, and filled with faith. You're in the greatest business in the world, that of *making* men and women. You're one of the lifter-ups of the world. Here —" The old man moved the book closer to the light of the table lamp, and began to read, his raspy little worn-out voice enunciating carefully:

" 'It is one thing to be lifting up the world from the earth side, it is another thing to be lifting up the world from the Heaven side. It is one thing to be a man on the earth living for the Glory, it is another thing to be a man in the Glory, living for the world. We must be taken out of the world first, and then sent back into it, to be any blessing to it. The reason Christ knew how to live was because He did not belong here. The Father had sent him from Heaven, and we must be sent from Heaven too, and work on earth as men that dwell in Heaven . . .' "*

_____
* A. B. Simpson.

The old man finished with a long half-groaning sigh, looked up at his favorite nephew. "You asked me a question. What was it?"

"I'm running in to town," Tim replied. "Have to mail a letter, and get the medicine for you. Is there anything you want?"

The old man frowned, shook his head. "Let me see — there was something. Well, never mind now. Maybe it wasn't important."

Tim turned, Bette Lu's letter in his hand, and went out to his maroon car.

At Dr. Mahone's office, that daintily mustached individual was surprised to see him. "Back again? There isn't anything wrong, I hope."

"Everything's fine. I just dropped in to get the capsules for Uncle John."

Young Dr. Mahone stared. "I—didn't I—?" he looked about him, his eyes scrutinizing his desk, the shelf above it where stood a row of bottles and cartons neatly labelled. Above that was a diploma from a widely known medical school . . .

And so Dr. Mahone came to know that there were twin brothers, and Tim came to know that Jim had been there thirty minutes before, and had taken Uncle John's capsules with him.

"I wonder," Tim said then, "if concentrated food like that wouldn't be good for anybody, to build them up. How about my taking some?" There was a strange pounding in his heart, while a stranger fear stormed there. Both fear and doubt. And the very center of the storm, the very cause of it, was his brother, who hated him with bitter hatred. A man who truly hated could do terrible things.

A little later Tim was driving back to the Nest. On the seat beside him was a carton of iron and liver concentrate, to be used by Uncle John in case Jim for any reason might forget. Oh this was a terrible thing to think about one's own brother! *Terrible!* He ought not to think it, and yet he could not help himself. He knew his brother too well.

―――――

The green car, carrying Jim, turned into the highway leading from the doctor's office, shot forward at top speed and was soon following the shore drive that bordered the wooded estate of John Sylvester Bishop. *And it is all mine,* he thought. When will it be all mine? *When* can I throw off the burden of debt? How long do I have to wait? As soon as Uncle John should die . . .

As soon! For the past month he had been failing fast, but today he had seemed more alive than ever. It was possible now, if Mahone's diagnosis was correct, that he might live a long time. Uncle John's heart was an old man's heart, but it was still beating. It was missing beats only, or *probably,* the doctor had said, because of his anemia. The oxygen carrying content of the blood was deficient.

"It may take a week or two to build his blood to normal — or we may not be able to do so. I have given him a *hypo* of iron compound with liver extract, and he is to take four of these —" The doctor had then produced a carton of brown capsules and handed them to Jim, — "four of these before each meal, for one week. But as I told him this morning, he's to do nothing strenuous."

"Four before each meal," Jim thought now as his car swung away and around the lake enroute to another destination.

For a moment, and for a long time after that, the driver of the green sedan listened, and kept on listening, to the voice of his mind which was suggesting, "If they're good for old men, they are also good for fishing!"

The miles flew past until the headlamps of his car showed him he was in the section of the resort territory where the wealthy had their summer residences. Here, amidst a network of paved avenues, were beautiful lawns set with exquisite shrubbery, flowers, and well-located trees, fountains and vine-covered trellises.

Some day, he told himself, the estate adjoining the Nest would be like this; but not until after he had sold it at his own price.

He swung his car into an arched drive marked "Private," and stopped beside a palatial home of English-Colonial architecture, as white as the Nest itself. The windows of the sunroom near which he parked, were trimmed in pale green. For a moment, before turning off his lights, he saw a wide sweep of lawn rolling down to the lake, saw green and white trellises covered with vines, luxurious outdoor furniture, the balusters of a stairway leading down to the dock, and farther out, the mast of a sailboat, with the sail furled, looking like a white ghost swaying to the accompaniment of the waves.

Far out on the lake were motor boats, with red, green and white lights, shooting hither and yon. To Jim's ears, as he stepped out of his car, came the sound of waves against the shore, like the rhythmic swishing of dancing feet in a mighty pavilion. There would be an up-to-the-minute dancing pavilion on the Grabill estate, with smoking rooms, luxurious lounging furniture, a soft-lighted cocktail bar with uniformed waitresses . . .

He made his way toward the red glow of a cigar at the top of the dock stairs. He was pleased to see that his man was alone.

"Martini?" he asked, when he was in speaking distance.

"That you, Grabill?" Martini's voice was gruff, abrupt. He indicated a deck chair beside him.

"Any news?" Martini asked. "How's your Uncle John's health tonight?"

"The old codger's got a new doctor. But I don't see how he can live much longer. . . . About that Cherryville property we were discussing — I've decided to accept your proposition and have you assign the mortgage over to me."

"You're in love with the girl, eh? Going to marry her?"

"Why not?"

Bailes Martini drew long and hard at his cigar. In the red glow of its fire, Jim saw the broad forehead, the long spatulate nose, looking as if it had been battered years ago in the fight ring. The man's body was short and stout, the muscles of his thick neck like those of a wrestler.

Again, the gruff voice, "What does the girl say about it? She in favor of it?"

"I don't want her to know. It's to be a surprise wedding gift."

"I suppose you want to charge it all to the — Nest? Three thousand dollars, you know. And there's back interest, which the girl's been working out. You'll have to run into the city Monday to my office. Can't just sign a thing like that. Have to go through with all the formalities: The law is very exact. Reads like this: 'Assignment must be executed by deed under seal, and acknowledged, delivered, and recorded with the same solemnity as attended the original conveyance.' You couldn't make it a wedding present though, unless you get married right away after you take over the mortgage. Have to give her mother notice of acquisition of title. You have to do that yourself. When's the wedding? Date set?"

"Not yet."

Martini stretched, yawned vociferously, relaxed in his deck chair, tapped the long ash from his cigar, gestured with it toward the lake, where high-speed motor boats roared at varying angles across the shimmering waters. "Look at that! Traffic out there's almost as bad as street traffic. Too d——— much noise! Fishing's no good for a mile along here. Have to drive clear across the lake to find a spot that's any good at all. Look at that, will you?"

A searchlight from a speed boat shot across the water, swung in a wide arc, struck the two men full in the face, and, for a too-long interval to have been unintentional, remained focused upon them. Bailes Martini exploded with an oath, threw up his arm to protect his eyes. The light beam flashed back to the lake, and the boat roared on up the shore.

"Younger generation's completely batty!" Martini commented, and turned his attention to the matter in hand. "Have a court case on Monday at nine. Drop into my office at two in the afternoon. By the way, you'd better dig up the three thousand somewhere —"

"But," Jim interrupted, "we have an agreement, don't we? I'm to sell you the eighty acres north of the cottage just as soon —"

"Business, my boy! Good business builds on foundations. Your Uncle John may live to be a hundred. And even if he'd die tomorrow, some relative might unearth himself and contest the will, and we'd have a long drawn-out suit. Nope! Can't depend on that!"

"I haven't three thousand dollars loose. It's all tied up in securities."

"I'll arrange a loan, if you like. Go on the note with you myself. 'Course you want to be sure you know your own mind. What if there's a slip between the cup and the lip? I mean, as far as this wedding business is concerned."

And Jim thought, "What if there is? *There already is!* I may have to use the mortgage to bring her to time." Yet he knew that love could not be forced. If he could in some way make it appear as if he were coming to the rescue, saving the Lane's from a foreclosure. . . . He would have to think that over. And if, in the end, he should lose Beryl, and if Timothy — Bah! *he makes me sick!* — if Timothy should win, it would be sweet to do the little foreclosing act. Next Monday afternoon, when the mortgage was assigned to him, the legal title to the Lane's fruit farm would be his. And some day he would have all the money he wished. He knew because Martini had said so. Six weeks ago he had learned the truth about the will. There had been the telephone summons to Bailes Martini's office, the private interview, and the advance information, given by Martini in short, abrupt sentences:

"Your Uncle made his will yesterday and you and your brother Timothy are the sole heirs. He's given you the Lake Crane estate, and his city property goes to Timothy. I have been trying to buy the Lake Crane estate for years, and the old codger wouldn't sell. *You* can make fifty thousand dollars on that property if you let me handle it . . ."

They had come to an agreement. Martini himself would buy the eighty acres next to the cottage, on the very day it came into Jim's possession. The Nest itself and twenty acres immediately adjoining on the other side, were to be retained by Jim.

A mere three thousand dollar loan would be nothing to pay back, and, at present, the Cherryville mortgage was essential to his plans.

They settled on an appointment in Martini's office in the city for Monday afternoon, and Jim arose to go. Standing, he saw, moored to the dock below, a gleaming, white runabout, with mahogany gunwhale and seats. Yesterday, he thought, Beryl had ridden away with Tim in old John's ancient dinghy; if tomorrow afternoon he could come gliding up to her dock with this dashing runabout, powered with a motor of large horsepower —

"That your runabout down there?" he asked Martini.

Martini growled an assent, flicked his cigar stub into the lake, came and stood at the head of the stairs beside Jim. There was a cool fifty-thousand dollars to be made from the old man's estate. If he could work things right, this little minnow of a youngster would make a good dinner for him.

"Like to take a little spin? Brought out a new Speeditwin motor 'safternoon. It'll do thirty miles an hour."

Jim looked ahead into tomorrow afternoon. Tim with his dinghy — Abel with his fleecy little lamb. What had Tim to offer except religion and drab, colorless living. The gleaming runabout, as compared to the weathered old dinghy — Timothy's mysticism, as over against Jim's dash and wealth — there would be money to burn.

"I'd like to take it for an hour or two tomorrow afternoon, if I may," Jim said.

And on that, also, they agreed.

On one thing, however, they disagreed.

"You understand, of course," Martini said, "that the war is going to be hard on business men. More taxes, and higher. Bigger business, probably, but only temporarily. When the thing's all over, there'll be the usual slump, and we're going to need plenty of reserve. Listen, Grabill, do you know what I'm doing by lending you thousands and thousands and getting nothing back but promises? I'll tell you what I'm doing. I'm making a great fool of myself! How do I know how long I'll have to wait until the funeral? What if the old man hangs on until you have to go off to train for some kind of war — which you're bound to have to do if you're single! Men die in wars, you know, Grabill. Then, where'll I be with all your unpaid notes in my possession?"

And Jim, feeling in his pocket the carton of capsules, remembering how essential they were to the health of the old man, thought again of the temptation that had come to him in the drive around the lake. He needed money badly, and he needed it now. He saw himself as a puppet in the hands of Lawyer Martini. *I am his tool!* He is making me — *driving me to do what I have to do!*

In his car, a little later, spinning back to the Nest, Jim studied his problem from every angle. He was already in debt to Martini for thousands. He was taking over the Cherryville property at three thousand more — at Martini's suggestion, and at his *insistence!* There seemed to be no other way out. Yet was it not the thing he wanted to do? That, now, was necessary to his own plans.

Over and over, the problem tossed about in his mind, tormenting him. He hated war; hated the thought of training and discipline and all that would be involved. And there was bound to be war again — world wide, probably. Martini said so. Leading American statesmen believed there would be. Uncle John claimed the Bible revealed there would be . . .

And yet there was no God, except as man had felt his need for one and had himself created him to suit his fancy. And yet again, why should a man feel his need for God unless Some Power had created that feeling. . . . Could a merely chemically controlled mind account for conscience? And why a conscience, if there were no Person to Whom to give account . . ?

Jim tossed from him the disturbing thoughts, and gave himself up once more to his problem: To simply toss the carton into the lake would solve nothing, for there was always more medicine in a doctor's office, and he would only be putting himself under suspicion. There would have to be some way out that would not involve danger to himself. . . . *Some other way!*

Fifty thousand dollars was a lot of money. It would wipe out every obligation to Martini. He could marry, if not Beryl, then someone else, and he would not be included in any possible war draft, in case America went suddenly insane on some defense program. Also, if not Beryl — if Tim should marry her — there would be sweet revenge in doing a little foreclosing on the Cherryville mortgage.

———

It was near midnight when Jim arrived at the Nest. He found his despised brother sitting near the fireplace, reading. "Here's Uncle John's medicine," he said. "I dropped in to Mahone's office and I guess he thought I was you. Anyway, he sent it out." He tossed the carton onto the radio table and went through the house to his own room in the rear. In his room he faced himself in the mirror. It had taken more courage than he had anticipated, but he had made himself do it. Rather, Martini had *driven* him to do it. His piled-up debts, the war-crazy world, the madness within him, had driven him to do it. *No! . . .*

The thought was a word; the word a shout! "NO! I am *not* responsible! I am a product of evolution! I have not yet evolved far enough on the upward trail." It was such an insignificant thing he had done, and it had been simple. The contents of the capsules had come out so easily. A little tapping and turning, one at a time. And they were filled now with a harmless substance of no medicinal value. The medical profession sometimes gave *placebo,* or bread pills to patients to humor them . . .

———

Timothy, watching his brother go to his room, his shadow cast by the firelight making a dark path for him to walk in, waited until he heard Jim's door close, then he lifted the carton, opened it. The capsules were the same as those in the carton from which an hour ago he had given the old man his first dose.

His conscience smote him that he should have suspected his brother of foul play, even though Uncle John's death would mean many thousands of dollars to them both. He stood, looking into the fire. He must not let Jim know he had doubted him, which he might do if he saw about the house a second carton. To destroy this might be a waste but —.

With a quick movement, he scattered the contents of the carton over the coals of fire, watched them until they were reduced to ashes, then he went up to his room, and to bed. Standing for a moment before the opened windows, the breeze from the lake blowing against his pajama-attired body, he vowed to himself one tremendous vow, "I will do everything in my power, even to the point of complete self effacement, to make him see Christ in me."

He lay upon the bed in the moonlight, watched the stars and the occasional cloud which drifted across the face of the moon. Tomorrow was the Lord's Day, and he, like John on the Isle of Patmos, would wish to be *in the Spirit,* for the Spirit was Christ's own Medium of revelation. In the morning there would be Sunday school and a service of worship in the little Finnish church of which Sprague was pastor. In the afternoon he and Beryl would go exploring again. What a beautiful island he had found! How out of tune he had been all these years, — and how much now he was enjoying his punishment — that of playing in tune. Or was he merely testing his instrument, restringing it, tuning it to the right pitch? After awhile there would be beautiful harmony.

After awhile.

13.

IT WAS two o'clock Sunday afternoon when the white runabout with Timothy Grabill's twin as the helmsman, came roaring across the bay, cut a wide circle in front of the dock, and came gliding to the beach.

Dora Jeanne, in modest blue gabardine play togs, the same as she had been wearing last night, heard the steady droning of the motor, as it grew louder and louder like an airplane riding out of the horizon and coming nearer and nearer — *swiftly*. "Airplane" was the half-formed thought that for a brief interval drew her attention from the book she was reading. She had been in a very dissatified mood since the morning sermon in the little Finnish church. The Reverend Hartford Sprague's theology had been too old-fashioned, she had thought, yet it had been the only sermon she had ever heard that had made her look straight into the mirror of the Book and see Dora Jeanne actually needing to be saved.

Afterward, she had been introduced to Hartford's Geneveve, had listened to her canary-like thrill, and had immediately liked her very much. Sunday school in the one-room church building had been a bedlam of voices, with six teachers trying to make ten times as many scholars hear the salient truths of the lesson. She had sat in Geneveve's class and listened to her talk radiantly about Christ, the Source of true contentment. The closing exercises of the Sunday school had been under Beryl's supervision, who, Dora Jeanne remembered, had been very efficient in that sort of thing back in Cherryville.

The sermon, following the same line of thought as Geneveve's talk to the class, carried a humble confession, and it was the very sincerity of it which had awakened Dora Jeanne. She knew she would never be able to erase its impressions — even if she had wanted to. Sprague's message had been:

104

"We, who are Christ's, are so united to Him in vital, *actual* relationship, that He is no longer an *external* Christ, doing things for us from the outside, but He is *within* us. He is the VINE and we are the branches. His life is actually, literally within us. We have been crucified with Him and it is no longer we that live, but Christ liveth *in* us.

"The spiritual life which we now possess, the eternal life, is not ours in any disconnected sense. Christ Himself *is* our eternal life. And since He has said, 'I came not to be ministered unto but to minister,' then as truly yielded believers in Him, we are no longer servants but friends. We are servant-branches, bearing the fruit which is the outflow of His life through us.

"Yesterday, Mrs. Sprague and I saw this truth in a beautiful way, yonder out in front of our cottage under a sandbar willow. While the waves washed against the shore, and the gulls squeaked overhead, we asked our Father to wash us clean from any selfish notion that we were doing great things for Him; we asked him there, my wife and I, to so control us that He Who came to minister, might be able to continue to do so *through* us, that everything we do in His name, may be done, not in our own strength but may be the fruit of His life within us ..."

And Dora Jeanne, hearing it, thought of how beautiful it was, and felt within herself a yearning to have that relationship as her own.

And now, lying in the hammock, reading, — trying to read — she felt a strange restlessness, and knew that it was not alone because she was without any saving relationship with Christ, but also, because she was a young woman, and was lonely for the companionship of a lover. Sunday afternoons at Cherryville had always been difficult, not because there were no young men, but because there were too many, none of which in any way compared with the dream man who some day would come to carry her away. The white-horse lover had so entangled himself in her thoughts that it seemed sometimes as if he had already come, and then had ridden away without her ...

With Beryl, he *had* already come. She and Timothy Grabill
had driven across the bay a half hour ago — *alone*, at Dora
Jeanne's insistence. "I want to cat-nap," she had told them.

———————

Suddenly alert, when the roar of the motor on the lake had
stopped, and she heard high waves washing against the dock,
Dora Jeanne sat up, laid aside the book, watched the man
balance his way toward the mahogany gunwale of the boat,
toss the anchor rope over a dock post, climb out and stand, six
feet tall, in white shirt and gray slacks, with light shoes. His
hair, a bit ruffled from the drive, was brown. In the sky behind and above him, the clouds were like a woman's white hair,
permanently waved, with patches of blue showing between the
waves.

Her heart turned a strange little somersault, and began to
sing. In the interval between the laying aside of her book and
the arrival of the tall Lochinvar at the porch steps, Dora
Jeanne heard fairies dancing on the roof on a rainy day, saw
life-sized dolls listening to stories of lovers on white horses,
saw a white horse lying dead under the old Sugar tree on the
farm at Cherryville, felt a springing up within her of an in-
explainable something which was hope and adventure and
dream-come-true and romance and thrill . . . All this in one
tumultuous emotion!

He was hatless, gallant, handsome. He was also the image
of Timothy Grabill. This was the twin about whom Timothy
on the way home from church had said, "Tim and Jim. We're
alike in every respect except for the first letters of our first
names, the color of our eyes and our dispositions." Beyond
that she knew nothing.

Dora Jeanne had liked *Tim* from the very first moment of
seeing him. She had thought how fortunate Beryl was to have
such a man so very evidently in love with her. He was that,
unless her ability to read gray eyes was only imaginary, and
she was glad for Beryl's sake. She had thought also with contempt of Cherryville and its colorless, insipid male population.

At the porch steps, Jim Grabill stopped, and in one sweep of his blue eyes — how *sky*-blue they were, Dora Jeanne thought, — brushed away all the musty melancholy of the past half hour.

She liked his handsome face, his touseled hair, his *sky*-blue eyes, his six feet of strength, his carefully tailored clothes, his white shoes, air-cooled with lattice perforations, his mock gravity, as he said — and she liked his voice —: "Is Miss Lane here?"

She hated her own rather feeble voice as she said with a smile which she felt was altogether too shy, "I suppose you mean Miss *Beryl* Lane. She's out motor-boating with —" She stopped, interrupted by the frown which creased his forehead.

"I know," he said, "I saw them over on the point. I just learned this morning that Beryl's very pretty sister is here visiting, so I've come to take her for a spin in my runabout — if I may?"

Hope, adventure, dream-come-true, thrill . . White horse . .
. . .

She hated herself for the blush she knew was crimsoning her cheeks — her *pretty* cheeks, — they were that, she knew — and said, "I'd planned to finish a book —" She picked up the book from the hammock, leafed through it slowly, hesitantly. She wanted more than anything else to go flying across the blue water with this man, who was the brother of Timothy Grabill and therefore must be a good and gallant and romantic gentleman. And he was older than the namby-pamby youths of Cherryville, who came storming up to the Lane residence on Sunday afternoons in battered old cars, bedizened with squirrel tails and ridiculous signs, like fledgling birds, learning to fly — O she was so tired of them all, with their inane pratings, their half-grown wit. She wanted glamour, romance, the things a man who was a man, could give! . . .

And Timothy Grabill's twin would be a *man*, different in disposition of course, as Tim had told her, but as courteous and refined; and with a smile that said, "Little Lady, I like you very much," and with eyes that said, "I have a lonely heart," he was laying himself at her feet in worship.

A few minutes later, the white-horse-runabout shot out from the dock and roared away, with James Grabill in the stern and with Dora Jeanne, on a brown leather, cushion-backed seat in front of him, facing the prow — facing *life!* Before her was a new world of thrill and adventure and romance. O, she had known, while she was back in drab Cherryville that somewhere in the world there was a *new* world for her. Cherryville, with its routine and canning and cooking and dusting and cleaning and getting up early in the morning and listening to Larry's gesticulated enthusiasms about this and that, — his seventeen old "setting" hens that were going to hatch two hundred fifty-five chickens, of which two hundred would live; his sixteen brood sows which, in a year's time, would contribute to the world's pig population, one hundred and seventeen wriggling, bright-eyed, curly-tailed spotted Poland China porkers; and, more shyly, and with enthusiasm that was smothered in bash-fulness, of his Lena, who like himself was seventeen, and unlike himself was graceful and gentle and soft-voiced. Good old Larry . . .

The wind caught at her hair, fine spray kissed her cheeks, dampened her lashes. The waves of white hair in the sky were like the ripples of the lake now, except for their color . . .

She swung her swivelled seat about so as to face him. The afternoon sun, in a patch of clear blue for a moment, hurt her eyes. She put on a pair of sun glasses, popularly advertised as "Daisy Sunglasses", with smoked lenses and a fringe of sun shade like the petals of a daisy, around the rim of each lense. The frames were white.

"Don't!" he said. "I can't see so well when you have them on!" Jesting, she thought, like the Cherryville boys — *boys!* But, coming from a man it seemed so different. She swung out into the current of his mood.

"Who's *doing* the seeing?" she asked. "Whose eyes are they?" She left the glasses on.

"You're asking *me?* Eyes like that can't afford to go about unclaimed."

And so it began.

Beryl and Tim had been standing high up on the crest of a promontory overlooking the bay, when Jim had gone racing past.

Jim had seen her evidently at the very instant she had seen him. For a moment his boat had swerved out of its course, and except for a quick movement of the steering handle, might have struck against the rocks, which, like a ridge of irregular vertabrae, pushed far out into the lake.

Tim, seeing, had stood beside her, grim-faced and silent, until his brother had disappeared up the shore. "Reckless, as always," he said as if to himself, then added, "Do you know what I decided last night, after our afternoon yesterday?"

He was not expecting her to reply, but only to wait for him to continue. Below them, to the right, and extending all the way to the Nest, marched a row of new birch, where years ago the waterline had been. Between the birches and the water's edge, was hard sand, in which cat-tails grew, their long sword-shaped leaves extending up and out like the fan-shaped trellises on the lawn in front of the Nest.

His voice was husky. "Knowing you," he said, "is going to mean I'll have to rewrite several chapters of my book."

She looked up at the drooping branches of the linden under which they were standing, picked a leaf, examined it absently. At night, in her cabin with the windows wide open, the fragrance of the linden's nectar-laden, creamy yellow flowers, was like honey. Last night, when for awhile she had lain awake, and the characters and episodes of her own book were playing at hide and seek in her mind, the perfume of the linden flowers had been sweet, as were also here thoughts of the man who now stood beside her . . .

"You see," he explained, and she noticed that the drone of Jim's motor had stopped. Jim was at her dock perhaps, and

he would see Dora Jeanne, and she him, and Dora Jeanne
would be swept off her feet in his first gallant introduction of
himself. It would be too much like her white horse vision of
which she had so often spoken in the past . . .

Her thoughts came back to Timothy, and broke into his sentence at the place where he was saying, ". . . I have never actually, seriously, tried to win Jim to Christ. I think I've been
more concerned about pruning him, rather than showing him
that he needs to be grafted into the Vine. *Now* I see, that if I
can, by God's Grace, get him vitally connected to Christ, in a
saving relationship, the pruning will take care of itself. Jesus
says in John 15, that the *Father* prunes the branches that are
in the Son and are bearing fruit, that they may bring forth
more fruit. It may be the Lord will have to prune me a little
too, so I can truly manifest Him to others, to Jim especially.
It's come to the place now, where he hates me —"

"The world hated Him 'without a cause,' " she quoted.

"True." He led her back to the rock at the very edge of the
promontory and seated her beside him. Below, playing in the
shallow water among the rocks, were summer ducks, known as
the wood duck. Many times he had stood here alone, he told
her, and had watched the ducks playing; and sometimes when
the wind swept across the lake and the waves dashed high,
crashed and broke against the rocks — "It does something to
a man," he ended, seemingly unable to express his emotions.
"It makes a man appreciate the beauty of — peace."

She was looking far out across the bay now. It was a beautiful location. No wonder, as Jim had said, millionaires were
trying to buy it. Soon, — as soon as John Sylvester Bishop
should die, — all this would belong to — whom? To Jim, or
to Tim? Evidently it was worth many times the "city property" mentioned in the lost codicil. Would the old man remember to have his lawyer come? she wondered.

And in the preparation of a new one, would he remember
the five thousand? Or would he, as he had promised, have

Tim draw the money from the bank for her. She wished she might confide in Tim at this very moment. It was too heavy a secret for her to carry alone . . .

"The wood duck," the man beside her explained, "is the most beautiful of all ducks in this territory. Ornithologists claim that it takes its specific name, *Sponsa,* which means *betrothed,* from its iridescence. Look at that big fellow over there on the rock! Green and purple and blue and every color of the spectrum."

Sponsa! *Betrothed!* He must not say things like that! It made her heart beat erratically, and it had no sensible right to do so, for she had not known him long enough. She did not in fact know him at all. A woman could not know a man until she had discovered all his moods — not only love, but hate and anger and gentleness — O, but he was gentle! And he was strong in character. And best of all he knew the greatest of all Lovers, the One Who had laid down His life, — and had taken it again. Timothy believed not only *about* Jesus; he believed *in* Him *experientially!*

He reached over, took the heart-shaped linden leaf from her hand, focused his eyes upon it. He did not speak for a full minute, then he said, "This is what I mean about making the change in the book I'm writing. See how beautifully it colors into your 'cold water' theory, and into Sprague's sermon this morning and into Geneveve's song — 'He is the Source of my Contentment' " —. He sang the first line, while she waited, fascinated. No man she had ever known had been able to talk to her of things that made her heart burn so strangely. What fuel was being heaped high upon her story fire for tomorrow's writing . . .!

"Notice, underneath the leaf, at the base of the stem, this little bract? Botanists call it a modified leaf, which it surely is, and it's a much lighter green. And here — See? Growing out of the central vein of the little bract, is the stem of the

flower cluster. Notice how securely it is attached, vitally connected, as Sprague pointed out this morning?

"Everything depends upon the connection. The life of the
tree flows out into the branches and through the branches
into the twigs, through the twigs into the stem of the leaves,
and through these ramified veins into every part of the leaf.
And here, so snugly and *vitally* connected to the main vein of
the little bract, is the stem of the flower cluster.

"*Everything* depends upon *vital connection,* and in its
finality, all the life depends upon the inflow of linden life
from the tree itself. The leaf is a linden leaf, because its inflow of life is linden. The creamy yellow flowers are linden
flowers because the inflow of life is linden. Their fragrance
is linden fragrance because their inflow of life is linden . . .

"And so, the most Christ-like man that ever lived, did *not*
say, 'For to me, to live, is *Christ-likeness,* but rather 'for to me
to live is *Christ!*'

"The cup of cold water which we give to others, is Christ
manifesting *Himself through* us. And as Sprague said this
morning, we are not ministering to others, but Christ, who
came to minister, is doing the work, bearing the fruit . . .
Beautiful, isn't it? . . ."

It was beautiful beyond anything she had known. Clearly
there came into her mind Dora Jeanne's words last night in
the north room of her cottage, "One would have to be fully
yielded to Him, wouldn't he? — to live that kind of life?"

They both sat up suddenly, for from across the bay came a
white runabout at high speed, spray dashing high on either
side. In the stern, as the boat came nearer and went roaring
past, the watchers on the edge of the promontory saw James
Grabill, and facing him, in blue play togs, a pair of Daisy sunglasses in her hand, sat Dora Jeanne. She was laughing and
listening as he waved his arm toward the shore in an explanatory gesture of some sort. Beryl waved a hand in salute to Dora
Jeanne but Dora Jeanne's eyes were turned again to the man

in the stern. A moment later, the white boat with its gleaming mahogany gunwhale was gone in a cloud of spray, around the point.

And in that moment Beryl felt a wild fear clutching at her heart. For in her mind's eye the beautiful white boat was a galloping white horse, and it was carrying away into a strange and dangerous land, her own vivacious, and pitifully innocent Dora Jeanne!

14.

THE week following was one of continued anxiety for Beryl, as she watched the progress of Dora Jeanne's whirlwind romance with Jim, which, however, was no more cyclonic than her own with Timothy.

On Monday Jim was away in the city on a matter of business, he told Dora Jeanne. He came back in high spirits, bringing a dozen Nigrette roses which Dora Jeanne set in a white vase on the porch table beside the lamp which had the blue sailboats on its shade. The roses, Beryl thought, were a deep maroon, the color of Timothy's car, their blackish-velvet sheen as soft as Dora Jeanne's velvety complexion.

Jim was so gallant and behaved himself so well, — and Dora Jeanne took on new beauty and was so happy, that Beryl did not have the heart to disillusion her. Yet it did not seem possible that the Jim Grabill she knew could have changed so abruptly and so very evidently into a new person.

She discussed it with Tim, and he said, "I've been giving him the cup, and I think — I don't know — it has made him thirsty for Christ. Let us wait and see what the Spirit does."

"But Dora Jeanne's being swept completely off her balance. It's her first affair, and she's giving it one hundred percent. She's such an impulsive creature — always has been —, that knowing Jim as I do, anyway, as he *was*, I've been afraid."

It did seem best however, to let things alone.

On Thursday afternoon, the fourth of July, Dora Jeanne, starry-eyed, hair windblown, cheeks glowing, came flying up the walk from a spin on the lake with Jim. "Quick, Beryl! Where's my shimmering stripe? Jim's taking the runabout back to Martini's dock, and in a half hour he'll be around in the car." They had been doing this all week, flying here and

there, roaring across the lake in Martini's flashy runabout,
with Dora Jeanne at the helm most of the time.

"We're driving over to sunset beach," Dora Jeanne exclaimed. "The Aquatennial's on there, you know — sailboat
regatta, swimming and diving contests —"

'There's dancing too, isn't there?" Beryl asked anxiously.
"You know —"

"Yes, I know how mother feels about that, —" Dora Jeanne
seemed a bit impatient — "but we're not dancing. Jim's given
it up, all on account of little me. He said so yesterday. Besides, you needn't think I'll ever let him take me in his arms,
even on a dance floor until I'm sure I love him."

"There's a lot of meaning in that little word *until*," Beryl
said. She was thinking of a time when for a selfish moment
she herself had been in Jim's arms — when he had argued the
prudishness of a woman wishing to give her love to one man
only, as long as she lived. It had been purely a selfish moment,
and a very disappointing one. Afterward her conscience had
smitten her mercilessly, saying, "You have committed sacrilege!
You have entered courtship's holy of holies with strange fire.
True love is the only rightful entrance to that sacred room;
you have sought to climb up some other way; you are a thief
and a robber!"

And from that wound's lesson she had resolved never again
to permit any man to caress her *until* true love bequeathed to
him the right.

Until. To Beryl the word recalled the past; to Dora Jeanne
it painted a radiant future. It therefore was to her a thrilling
present. It was the symbol of something deep and fine, which
only a good man could give.

Dora Jeanne dashed from dressing mirror to wardrobe to
bureau drawer, to the mirror again. "Like this new hair-do?"
she asked, bob pins between her teeth. "Jim's crazy about it."

The blue eyes which Beryl saw in Dora Jeanne's mirror were
those of a girl caught in the whirl of her first love. The disillusionment, which, if Jim ran true to form, was bound to

come, would crush Dora Jeanne's heart, unless, of course, Jim had actually changed. Timothy had advised, "Let them alone awhile," and Timothy's judgment was good. He was trying to give the cup.

Beryl tucked her book manuscript away in its file, rolled the drawer shut. There would be no more writing to-day. Timothy was coming in an hour anyway and they were driving over to the regatta themselves. It would furnish a new scene for her story — to see scores of white sails on the lake, like as many great white gulls with uplifted wings, playing in the water — like wood ducks among the rocks — *Sponsa* — *Betrothed!* If Dora Jeanne's emotions were like her own, it would seem tragic to be disillusioned. Perhaps Jim was actually going to change — had already done so. Yet could any change for the better be genuine unless it was an *inner* change? A house without a foundation must eventually fall . . . Dora Jeanne had a way, and she was lovely in her new shimmering stripe dress, modestly cut. Dora Jeanne, for all her gaiety and her love of beautiful clothes, was always modest. Perhaps it was her one hundred percent wholesomeness that was influencing Jim . . .

One question, however, Beryl had to ask. "You're going to be sure you know all about him before you let yourself fall in love, aren't you? — *Dora Jeanne!* Look at me! I'm desperately serious about this. I don't want you to be swept along too fast. There are many angles, you know —"

There *were* many. Dora Jeanne had discovered a new one, which she proceeded to explode at that very instant. She spoke through the mirror. "Of course you know that his Uncle John has willed him the Nest and one hundred acres of lakeshore property; and you know that the Lanes, back in stuffy little old Cherryville have a mortgage of twenty-five hundred dollars on their little farm; and you know also that it's going to come due next September first. You know all that, don't you? And that Mother has only about five hundred dollars saved toward paying it off? Aren't you tired of drawing only half salary from Martini — the old skinflint! — and wouldn't you like to be free to write all you want to and become a famous novelist? And wouldn't Larry and Lena be thrilled to pieces to spend a carefree summer vacation at the Nest with Mr. and *Mrs.* James Grabill! Don't worry, Berylie girlie, little Dora Jeanne knows how to feather her own Nest! I'm going to rush right in where an ordinary angel would fear to tread!"

So that was it! Exaggerating Jim had told her of dazzling summers in the Nest at Lake Crane, moonlit nights in Hawaii, lazy afternoons in sunny Mexico . . . *After* Uncle John was dead!

"And on top of that, —" Dora Jeanne whirled around from the mirror and faced her older sister triumphantly, — "Tonight Jim's taking me over to millionaire row, and we're going to watch the fireworks display from the lawn of — believe it or not! — old Bailes Martini himself. Jim has a little business matter to talk over with him. And you can believe this or not, but while the rest of the world's been sleeping, I haven't. And neither has Jim. He's found out that old Martini was going to foreclose on us, — and what did he do? He walks into Martini's office in the city last Monday afternoon, bearded the lion in his den, and not only talked him out of it, but actually had him assign the mortgage over to him —"

Beryl gasped. "He — *what!*"

"Inveigled Martini into assigning the mortage over to him. Jim had him over a barrel, so to speak. Martini's been trying to buy about eighty acres of the property that belongs to Uncle John and Uncle John wouldn't sell. Then a few weeks ago, out of a blue sky, Uncle John has Martini help him draw up his will, and lo and behold Jim's to get the Nest and everything that goes with it, so that's the way the cyclone has been moving. You and I are being swept along in the very center of it, without even knowing it. Jim's wonderful to take care of things like that for us, don't you think?"

Think! Beryl couldn't. For a moment her thoughts became a confusion of wills and mortgages, lost codicils, Jim and Tim, identical twins, spatulate snouted great northerns lying in wait for the unwary, temperamental walleyes, nibbling at every passing bait. Jim was playing a serious game this time. Too serious for others in the game to go to sleep on the job. Was he doing all this because he loved adorable little Dora Jeanne? Or was it in the spirit of revenge — against both Beryl and Tim? She recalled the afternoon last week when she and Tim were on the promontory above the rocks, watching the ducks playing. Tim had said, "It's come to the place now where he hates me —"

And she had replied to that, "The world hated *Him* 'without a cause.' "

And whosoever hateth his brother, *is a murderer,* the One who knew the hearts of all men, had declared.

Jim *wonderful?* He would never be that. But if all this were true, there was a cyclone indeed, and she and Dora Jeanne and Timothy and all of them were in its center; there was a *whirlpool* and they were in its *vortex!*

Dora Jeanne, who had turned back to the mirror again, now whirled about impatiently. "What's the matter, Ber? What'd I say? You look like you'd seen a ghost!"

"I — I'm afraid I have." Beryl suddenly stood, went out onto the porch, looked across the blue lake to the Nest and to the little sun room on the roof, Tim's writing room. He was there now, perhaps, winding up his work for the day, getting ready to drive around the lake for her. She wished he were here; she felt her need of him . . . *So, I am the efficient business woman who never goes to pieces, who never needs a lover's soothing voice to comfort her, or a strong pair of arms in which to seek refuge!* If only she could fly to him now and tell him everything!

And then, all in a flash, James was there with his car. She heard him stopping in the drive beside the cottage, heard his car door open and his footsteps in the gravelled path.

Smiling, bare-headed, in immaculate white and gray, wearing white, lattice cooled shoes, he swung around the corner of the cottage. He stopped abruptly when he saw Beryl.

"Dora Jeanne ready?" he asked, and bowed to Beryl as if to a mere acquaintance.

"Ready!" Dora Jeanne chirped, enroute from the living room to the porch. She swished through the door, past the lamp with its blue sails, her satiny striped dress shimmering like the lake under a moon.

Beryl saw two pairs of blue eyes meet: the one, dreamy, trusting, a-sparkle with youthful vivacity; the other showing admiration, and something more, something — what was it? It was certainly deeper than admiration.

Dora Jeanne tossed a gay little "Bye!" to Beryl, and went out to Jim. "Be back to-night sometime!" she called over her shoulder. "Don't wait up for me."

Hurriedly, Beryl turned back into the cottage, through the living room and into the north wing, to watch them drive away. She had never seen Dora Jeanne when she was more attractive. She was no longer the gay little dreamer of her girlhood days, but a young woman whose dream was coming true — and what a dream! With what terrible disillusionment she would awaken!

Beryl was seized for a moment with the desire to scream! To rush madly out to them and tell Dora Jeanne the whole truth about James Grabill as she knew him — that he made love to every pretty girl he met. That he could not know himself whether he was in love, because he was incapable of knowing. He would never be able to pay the price of holding the love of a woman, once he had won it. It was Dora Jeanne's pretty face that had captivated him —

Or was it Dora Jeanne herself? There had been *something* in his eyes that was like the love-light she had seen in Tim's eyes that day on the promontory. And if it were true — the things those eyes had said, then what right had she, Beryl, to interfere?

Gallantly, he swept Dora Jeanne into the luxurious front seat, closed her door, circled the car and slid in beside her under the steering wheel.

One spoken word came clear and unmistakable to Beryl's ears. She knew she had heard aright, because had she not heard it herself on another occasion? It was: "Love me?" and was accompanied by a playful hand twitching her chin. That gesture also was familiar and brought with it certain memories . . . "No, Jim, I don't!" she had told him herself that night.

"And why not?" he had wanted to know.

Her answer had been sufficiently explanatory, "Because I don't." A woman either did or didn't . . .

But now, with Dora Jeanne being asked the same question, things were different. She fancied she could hear her happy little sigh as she chirped an indistinguishable reply, which Beryl, with a heavy heart, interpreted to be, "A little." It could have been that, although Dora Jeanne, for all her impulsiveness, was not the type to admit things until she was very sure — climactic things, such as love.

The man under the steering-wheel seemed satisfied, for he gave Dora Jeanne's demure little chin a second playful twitch, spun the motor. The green car leaped forward, disappeared down the drive . . .

Dead to Jim . . . Alive to Tim. The one had bidden high — offering to Beryl things which now were not his to offer — according to the lost codicil, and also according to the new one Uncle John Bishop had planned to make . . . And now Jim was bidding high for Dora Jeanne!

Once in the long ago, a Man, filled with the Spirit, had stood immovable under the temptation — *"All this will I give, if Thou wilt fall down and worship me."* That same Man, Jesus, had returned from the temptation *"in the power of the Spirit."* (Luke 1:14).

If only Dora Jeanne were Spirit-controlled, she would be safe. If only she could know His guidance!

Slowly, in deep reverie, Beryl turned from the window to her mirror. Her eyes were troubled. The problems confronting the characters of her story had lifted themselves from the pages, and were tormenting the author. They had become her very own. Satan was reaching out his tentacles to clasp Dora Jeanne. She knew — *knew* that Jim was only acting. And yet, if his seeming change *were* genuine, —!

It was too much for a mere stenographer to solve. She turned from the mirror, and fighting the hot tears that blinded her eyes, she went to the drawer where her manuscript was kept, and with it in her hands, she clasped it to her bosom. Both she and Timothy had been more than kind to Jim, had gone beyond even the "second mile," and there was no reward — only that he was stealing away from her precious Dora Jeanne, and would break her heart. She *knew* he would, unless — unless the God of Heaven intervened. Surely doing the "extra" thing must be correctly interpreted or one could be misled. *One could cast his pearls before swine . . .*

The green grass rug upon which she knelt was cool to her knees while she prayed. And then, the Spirit coming upon her, she lifted her eyes toward the ceiling, extended her manuscript up and out in a gesture of dedication, and sobbed to Him Whom she loved so tenderly, "O my Father, guide me in the writing of the rest of it! Let me place no false interpretation upon Thy Word. And — Father — hold Dora Jeanne in the hollow of Thy hand today. I do not ask Thee to spare her all pain, for pain may be temporarily Thy servant to save her from ruin, but I do ask Thee to overrule the deeds of the ruler of this world, Satan. I ask in the all-conquering Name of Thy Son, MY Saviour, the Lord Jesus Christ. Amen."

Arising from prayer, she stored the manuscript away in its file, locked the drawer. Soon Timothy would be here — Timothy with his mysterious gray eyes, his gentle wit, his tenderness and his Gibraltar faith. It did not seem possible that she — *little me, stenographer* — should be loved by so great and good a man. Philosopher, student of "the general laws that furnish the rational explanation of anything," he had told her one day this week, "Character is what one *does;* what one *does* is what one *thinks;* what one *thinks* is what one *is;* what one *is,* is what he allows God to make him. The only truly lovable things in any one's character are those which are Christ-implanted — That's why I like you, Beryl."

He had said *like.* His eyes had said "love." One, she knew, was essential to the other. Love alone might be blind, but if one could both *love* and *like,* that was love with its eyes open.

Ready and waiting for him to come, Beryl dashed off a letter to Mrs. Schaeffer:

"Timothy, about whom I told you in my other letter, will be here in a few minutes, and we are driving over to Sunset Beach to the Aquatennial. He is so humble and child-like in his faith, yet so like one of God's giants.

"Of course you are wondering how my story is progressing. I think I can say truthfully, however humbly, that it will some day prove a blessing to many. I do have days when the plot seems all in a tangle and my mind is so sluggish, but after a period of rest or recreation, or after a good night's sleep, I am caught up in a veritable whirl of ideas, and the little old typewriter roars away for hours without stopping except when I have to search for the right word or do a bit of *re*search in order to be authentic. I have learned also a secret which is making it easy to go back to work, after rest, and that is, never to stop writing except at an interesting place. When I do that, my characters are like powerful magnets, pulling me back to them . . .

"It seems to me now, as I write this, and while the dear Holy Spirit is making the presence of God so real, that I must have been fore-ordained to this work. — And now here comes Timothy — Professor Timothy Grabill to you — and please forgive my impertinence —."

Beryl tucked the letter in a drawer, and a moment later was ready. She knew by the way his face lit up when he met her at the screen door that he liked her outfit — the white sharkskin again, hair tucked into blue snood, her bright red jacket,

— all in keeping with Independence Day. He was wearing gray and white, with white shoes.

Big Sam Grady strolled over to see them off. "You two youngsters get in early tonight!" he commanded in his usual playfully gruff tone. "Molly and I can't sleep when our children are out late. Everything locked up, Miss Lane? Fourth o' July's always a bad time for house-breaking. Thieves know everybody's likely to be 'way from home."

"Here's my key." Beryl handed her key ring to him. "That's the key to my files," she said, indicating a smaller one.

A little later they were off with only one cloud to darken the day's sky. That cloud was one that threatened high winds and a violent storm, which might break even before the day was past.

15

SINCE the day they had explored the little island, Timothy had been exploring with growing delight, the fertile mind of the demure little lady who now sat beside him in the maroon car, as they followed the winding trail of the drive along the lake shore.

The voice of his own desires had cried loudly during the past week, saying, "This, at last, is the girl for whom you have been waiting." But he could not be satisfied to know merely that he was in love. "In love" was an *effect*. He must know also the *cause*. *Why do I love this gracious girl with the blue eyes, the calm spirit, the fervent love for the Lord Jesus?* . . .

The drive, which was little more than a lane — a winding Lane to be explored! — trailed its way through oak and linden and balm of Gilead and Indian cherry. Here and there, in secluded nooks, nestled summer cottages, each with its own dock leading out or down to the lake itself. There were few bathers here today, for the Aquatennial at Sunset Beach had drawn the crowds there.

Well, little lady, he thought, today will be the supreme test for you. If you pass today's examination, this professional old heart of mine will surrender its last fortification. You will have stormed my last remaining citadel. But if you don't —! Well, why did students fail to pass examinations anyway? Could not an instructor himself be to blame, at times, for not preparing his students?

They did not talk at first. Contentment did not require conversation. Also he was a bit disturbed because he thought he had noticed a trace of tears in her eyes when he had first greeted her at the porch steps.

Rounding a shaded bend at the head of the lake, the lane swerved sharply to the left, climbed at an abrupt angle and came out into a clearing, dotted with a number of alike cottages, each with a neatly kept wide green lawn. At the crest of a knoll, overlooking the lake, was a weathered ice house, with sawdust scattered profusely about its battered wooden door. Straight ahead, isolated and looking a bit lonely, stood a neat little white church building, above the double-door entrance of which in Old English were the words:

THE LITTLE WHITE CHURCH
ON THE HILL

Sensing plot material when she saw an explanatory bulletin board on the lawn, Beryl asked Tim to stop. She slid out of the car with an absent-minded "Excuse me," and a moment later was copying into her notebook the data on the bulletin board.

"Absent-minded professor," he thought, and chuckled to himself. She too was going to be mentally abstracted. But they would both emerge from their other worlds long enough each day to appreciate each other and to enter into each other's thoughts and activities . . .

From the parsonage next door, a bespectacled little gentleman came out and stopped at the car. He looked at Timothy over the tops of his half-lens glasses and queried, "Weddings?"

And Timothy, looking over the minister's shoulder at the red, white and blue little lady standing by the bulletin board, blushing as furiously as when he had accused her of having stolen his love, wished it were.

In a moment she was at the car. The courteous minister bowed in recognition, as she explained, "I've been stealing information from your bulletin board, that's all."

They thanked him and drove off.

"Too bad to disappoint him," Timothy remarked as they turned again into the winding shore drive.

She was giving attention to her notebook. She had heard what he said, but she wanted to hear it again, — "I beg your pardon?"

"I say, I think the little minister really had his heart set on a wedding. It's too bad to have disappointed him. He probably needed the fee." He was talking lightly, yet he knew the water was running deep under the rippling surface.

"I'm sorry, too, but I wasn't in the mood. However, I believe I shall have the hero and heroine in my story go there. Don't you think that would be ideal?"

"Listen," he heard himself saying, as they waited at a stop sign at the highway entrance, "if you don't quit stealing things, such as information from church bulletin boards and — words —, I'm going to take you to a place like that and have it stopped once for all."

"Before, or *after* I've returned what I've stolen?"

"When Zacchaeus in the New Testament was converted he restored things four-fold."

That had been a radiant night — there on the porch with the Spragues, watching the lonely little moon, talking of the deeper things of the Spirit — swinging lightly from one theme to another — driving back across the bay with Beryl, — and at her dock, when she had fallen, or would have, — that night had been climactic for him. He had been living in a new world ever since. Some day it would be his privilege and right to have this girl as his very own — that is, — he checked his wish-thoughts — *if* she passes today's test.

At Sunset Beach they parked at a previously-arranged-for place, near a cottage owned by one of the members of Sprague's church. From their vantage point at the crest of a knoll they could watch the regatta, yet be alone. Tim spread rugs for them in the shade of a sprawling linden. Below rolled the long white beach, dotted here and there with little willows and baby birch. They were far enough away from the center of things — the great Midway, with merry-go-rounds, ferris-wheels, refreshment stands, gambling booths, side shows of a score of teasing varieties, each with a barker vociferating the superiority of his particular brand of entertainment —, yet they had a clear view of the lake, where the sailboats were racing — *crawling,* rather. For except for wandering breezes which ruffled the waters in isolated places, there was no wind, and the boats were motionless most of the time.

"Look!" Beryl exclaimed suddenly, "See that little white boat with the cross on its sail! It's moving ahead of the rest." A vagrant wind had moved in from across the lake, had caught the sail of the little boat and was pushing it swiftly along.

But it was only for a moment. Other winds moved here, there, added their bit to the occasion, then lifted, or died away.

"Have you ever sailed?" Tim wanted to know. He brushed a black ant from the sleeve of her red jacket.

"Never."

"Want to?"

"Very much."

"Sprague's been making a sailboat in his spare time. Everything's finished now except the rudder. As soon as he gets it hinged on, you and I shall go sailing. And whichever way the wind blows, that's the way we go — drifting, sailing along — only you'll have to trust me —"

"That'll be my big problem — not that there's anything wrong with my faith, but a person has to be careful where he invests his faith. Faith is an investment, you know. And if the market should —"

"I know, I know —don't say it!" They were saying so much, and thinking so much more.

Crowds . . . crowds . . . They could see them farther down the shore, jostling, laughing, spending. . . . Hundreds of people . . . thousands . . . like sheep having no shepherd — and not wishing any; for many of them would rather be astray than in the fold, or in the Shepherd's pasture. Only those who had come to love the Shepherd, knew the sordidness of life without Him . . .

Tim lifted his bare brown arm, noticed that his wrist-watch indicated half past three. It was time now for the beginning of the final test.

And then, unannounced, Hartford Sprague and his Geneveve were there, laughing, exclaiming with feigned surprise at finding Beryl and Tim.

Geneveve availed herself of a corner of Beryl's rug, accepted a pillow, sighed a happy tired sigh, and relaxed. "It's getting hotter and hotter down there, but I've made up my mind I won't quit until we've given out every last one of them. Even at that we won't have enough. Listen, you two! When those snails out there get to the end of their race — or sooner, as far as I'm concerned — I want you over to the cottage. There's ice cream in the trays and six nice juicy walleye waiting to be fried. There's going to be a moon again — it's getting larger all the time — growing faster than that squash in the garden — and we'll finish the game of Anagrams we started last time ——"

He needn't have worried himself in the least as to Beryl's not passing the test. She passed it with flying colors, the very moment she saw the neat little cellophane rolls of gospel tracts which Hartford and his Geneveve had been distributing to the crowd. A printing company in the city had furnished the tracts, already rolled in varicolored cellophane, in each roll a beautifully printed series of choice Christian tracts ready for distribution.

The red, white and blue lady — *and gold!* — Tim thought, was not only thrilled with the possibilities of getting out the Good News to so many in such a unique way, but she was alert to have an immediate part in their distribution. Consequently, as soon as Geneveve had rested all she would allow herself to, she and Beryl were off, with a basket of tracts swinging on Geneveve's arm, the tracts in their cellophane wrapping looking like colored diplomas.

"Tim and I will take the scattered sheep along the beach," Sprague told them, "and we'll meet you here when we're through."

Standing under the linden, the leaves of a lower branch tousling his hair, Tim watched the receding pair — "Jenny" in blue, with a white hat at a cheery angle; Beryl in Independence Day colors. His throat tightened for a moment, and he was thrilled with a beautiful emotion as he thought, "Grand little Lady! not only unashamed of the gospel, but actually proud to be a soldier for Him!"

They were watching together, these two men, watching and thinking — and planning, perhaps. Then Hartford said, "Jenny and I were talking this morning, and we decided that as far as we are concerned, our minds are already made up. Of course we wouldn't wish to exert any undue influence over you, but Jenny knows gold when she sees it; and that little red, white and blue lady yonder is one in a thousand — There! Look at that, will you? See her give out that roll to the lady in the fortune teller's booth? Why — O, pardon me! It does get into a fellow's heart, doesn't it . . ?"

It *had* gotten into his heart — and into his throat. And now it was in his eyes. Tim turned away, smothered a sob, and said under his breath, "O Father-God! Make me worthy!"

16.

DORA JEANNE, happy as she had never been in all her life before, looked with dreamy eyes out across the lake to where the white sails glistened in the sun. The man beside her, on the rug taken from his car, was spinning word pictures of a future in which there would be travel, beautiful clothes, a luxurious home with servants; social prestige — "anything in the world your little heart may wish."

They had found a secluded nook in a clump of baby birch in the sands near the shore. There Jim had spread his rug, and there, sheltered from the eyes of chance observers, they sat and talked, and Dora Jeanne argued with her own heart in vain. This at last was love. It had come like a flood and was carrying her away, and she did not care where, if only the beautiful whirl of things could continue . . .

The spinning went on — "First thing I'll do after our honeymoon, is to wipe out the mortgage on your old home, and establish a trust fund for your brother, Larry, so he can go to college. — He'll go to the State University, of course. I went there, you know. You and I'll take a plane to somewhere — maybe to old Mexico, or to the Grand Canyon. Then California and Catalina Island. There's a fourteen-day tour into the Scenic Southwest that takes in all those places: Grand Canyon — plane follows the Canyon for over one hundred and fifty miles — best way in the world to see it — Boulder City, Phoenix, Los Angeles. There's a week stopover at a ranch near Phoenix, with horseback riding. They have the most beautiful white horses there, —"

For a moment Dora Jeanne's thoughts were astray. She was back in Cherryville on a rainy day, with the attic door open, with fairies dancing on the roof; fierce lightnings played grimly; terrific thunders crashed, hissed, roared and rolled in violent reverberations across the sky; and then, out in the pasture under the big Sugar tree, she and Beryl found the six horses, *dead,* sprawled across each other in a horrifying heap; and Jim, her favorite white horse was dead too! *JIM! God had killed him!* . . .

She shuddered and drifted back to the present. The man on the rug beside her, looking down into her eyes, had reached out a soft hand and taken hers, and she was letting him hold it. What was he saying now? Her heart was pounding so. "Remember the little white church we passed back there just off the highway? We could be married there and surprise everybody. No one needs to know about it anyway. I'll call the airport and make reservations, and we'll be off."

He was saying it so calmly, so — almost indifferently — as if he didn't care. O how controlled he was! When her own emotions were like a — like a terrible storm! . . .

He was making her look into his eyes now — his blue, *blue* eyes, like the sky yonder above the lake. She was going to say — O, what was she going to say! He was so handsome! So in earnest! . . . And yet, wasn't it too soon for him to be asking her! . . .

She heard voices farther up the beach. . . . "I'll get those two under the birches, and then we'll be through." She heard footsteps coming across the sand.

Dora Jeanne, startled out of her dream world, withdrew her hand from Jim's, and with her thoughts twisted into a crazy sort of knot, waited for the man to appear.

"Someone's coming!" she said, as if in apology. She *had* to have time to think, and this perhaps was her opportunity. Airplane! Old Mexico! Grand Canyon! A week at a Guest Ranch in Arizona! White horses — *WHITE* horses! . . . Larry going to college! The mortgage on the old home wiped out! Beryl free to follow her true life work! And all this hinging on one little word, *"Yes!"*

In a moment whoever was coming would have come and gone, and she would be alone with her lover again, and he would expect her answer.

And then, without warning she was seeing double! Jim was coming across the sand, smiling, making straight for their little rendezvous! Jim was also reclining on one elbow beside her!

She heard Jim curse under his breath, felt his anger rising as surely as if it had been her own.

"Good afternoon," Timothy Grabill said cheerfully. "We're distributing diplomas to everyone at the Aquatennial — a little souvenir, and an invitation to a Great Supper — Oh, *hello!* Is *this* a sur*prise!*"

Dora Jeanne saw the scowl on Jim's face deepen.

Tim hesitated. In his right hand were two little cellophane rolls, one purple and the other gold. "We've been looking for you," he said. "The Sprague's have invited us all to their cottage for a fish-fry tonight. A fish-fry and a moon-watch."

"Is that all?" Jim asked. "Sorry, but Miss Lane and I are watching the fireworks display over on Pillsbury. What have you there? Stick candy?"

Dora Jeanne saw Timothy stiffen, as if a bullet had struck him.

And Timothy, looking into the angry eyes of his brother, reading in them the history of many years of dislike for him, feeling the rebellion in his mind against the Gospel, felt his own anger rising like a hedge of thorns between them. He wanted to retort with sharp words. *Stick candy!* Jim knew what was in the cellophane rolls! Tract distributors in the city used them freely!

And Dora Jeanne, looking up at him questioningly. Did she feel the tenseness of the atmosphere? he wondered. On which side of this wordless battle were her sympathies? . . .

All this flashed through his mind with lightning speed. He checked his thoughts. He would never win his brother by meeting anger with anger. He must go the extra mile, give the *cup . . . again and again!*

"Sweeter than stick candy," he said. "It's the very Word of God, of which the Psalmist says in Psalm one hundred nineteen: one hundred three, '*How sweet are Thy words unto my taste! yea, sweeter than honey to my mouth.*'"

With that, Timothy extended the cellophane rolls to Dora Jeanne who accepted them. "And *this*," he said, "I almost forgot. I stopped at the post office on the way over, and they were putting out the mail." Tim fished a gray envelope from a pocket, handed it to Jim. "No bad news, I hope," he said, turned and went up the beach.

Alone again, the two under the shade of the birches knew that things between them were not as they had been a few moments ago. The atmosphere was tense. Dora Jeanne's eyes were upon the pearl gray envelope in Jim's hands, and at which he was staring curiously. The handwriting was that of a woman. *Another* woman! Dora Jeanne's jealous heart told her when she saw the name in the upper left hand corner: *Bette Lu Rhinestone.*

Rhinestone! That was the name of the — where had she seen the name before? In the newspapers? In the society columns?

"If I may?" Jim said, and tore open the envelope. A little booklet tumbled out upon the rug, and lay face up. A gold stamped title on the fabrikoid cover said:

THE
BEST THING
IN LIFE

She watched his face while he read, saw the sneer that stencilled itself about his lips. The letter was brief, written on two pages only. He finished it, and with a gesture of contempt tossed it to Dora Jeanne, saying, "Just a rich girl who once thought she liked me. Read it if you wish." He picked up the tiny booklet and leafed through it.

"Sure you wish me to — read this?" she asked.

"If you can stand it. In fact, I think you'll find it very coincidental — that letter and this — stick candy!"

Dora Jeanne read:

"My Dear James:

"Yesterday I read a very clever little short story entitled, "A Cup of Cold Water," which was not only clever, but had a tremendous wallop in it. It made me realize that although I am a Christian — have been ever since my first term at Phillips College, thanks to your twin brother, Tim, — I have been far too indifferent to the spiritual needs of those who are or have been in my own immediate circle.

"For this reason, I am enclosing a very attractive little booklet, *The Best Thing In Life,* which, I think you will agree with me, is not only beautifully gotten up, but is one hundred percent true.

"Listen, Jim, I have truly found the best thing, and I want everybody to know it. . . . It is only a little cup I am giving you, but it has LIFE in it, Jim, and I shall pray that you may drink . . ."

Dora Jeanne finished the letter with mingled emotions. Who was Bette Lu — that is, how intimately did she and Jim know each other? Was it perhaps Beryl's own short story that had awakened her? O, Beryl must be unshackled from all other responsibilities that she might write . . .

"And here," Jim said, "is the cold water — somebody's always throwing cold water on my plans. This is the sort of stuff my beloved brother, Timothy, is wasting his time on." Dora Jeanne watched him light a cigarette, toss the match away. There was something — was it repulsive — in the way he tossed away the match? In the toss of his head as he dismissed his brother Tim . . . ?

It was a very neatly printed little booklet, printed in two colors — red and black, with five full-page photographs which, the last page said, were taken with a Rolleiflex camera.

And while Jim smoked and she waited for the atmosphere to clear between them — the smoke of battle between brother and brother — Dora Jeanne looked through the little two by two and one-half inch booklet:

Page one: In large letters, THE BEST THING IN LIFE:

Page two: "Is Not *Pleasure*."

Page three, directly across from page two: a full-page photo of a man on skis.

Page four: "Is Not *Success*."

Page five, directly across from page four: a full-page close-up of a successful looking business man.

Page six: "Is Not *Health*."

Page seven, directly across from page six: a full-page photo of a beautiful child in robust health.

And then came pages eight and nine, ten and eleven. The Best Thing in Life was not Wealth or Wisdom . . .

Jim was still smoking, and re-reading the letter from Bette Lu.

The best thing in Life, declared page twelve in startling type, is *"TO BE SAVED!"* The remaining four pages told *What* and *How*. The atmosphere was still heavy. Startlingly, the thought came to her: To Jim, the best things in life were pleasure, success, health, wisdom, and wealth. And to Dora Jeanne, what were they? Certainly not *To Be Saved!*

He finished the letter once more, folded it, and slowly tore it to shreds. He took the gold cellophane-wrapped "souvenir," struck a match, touched it to the end, and tossed it far out onto the sand of the beach.

Numbed, not understanding the inertia within her, Dora Jeanne watched him do the same to the second roll. She was thinking of Beryl and Tim and of Bette Lu Rhinestone who had found the best thing in Life. *LIFE!* They had found life itself. It flowed from the VINE into each of its branches, as Beryl had been telling her, but one would have to be grafted in first. Until then, one was — one was — *Dead!*

Out on the sand two little colored torches were smoldering. Jim reached out now for the fabrikoid booklet.

Without knowing she was going to react so violently, Dora Jeanne pushed his hand away, stiffened. The very touch of his hand was repulsive. The man himself was repulsive! His handsome, smooth-shaven face was the face of a — the thought came like a flash — like a *lightning flash* — *it was the face of a dead man!* JIM . . . DEAD! GOD HAD KILLED HIM! Rather, God had killed with one stroke Dora Jeanne's love. . . . She was seized with an impulse to run away.

She was on her feet, the little booklet in her hand. She was running. Running and crying and carrying a great big lump of heartache that was like death itself.

Old Mexico! Grand Canyon! Honeymoon! College for Larry! A week at a Guest Ranch in old Arizona! WHITE HORSES! . . .

He called after her, but she did not stop. She could not. She *would* not! Up the beach, her steps dragging heavily in the sand, her shimmering dress like a runaway rainbow, she hurried. She was running away from pleasure and wealth and romance and social success and — disillusionment. And O, she did not want to be disillusioned! But he had ridiculed the things she believed in. The things her mother believed in. And Beryl and the Spragues and Timothy and — and he had ridiculed God Himself!

Ten minutes later Dora Jeanne came unexpectedly upon a little lane, and on the other side of it, flowing parallel to it, a tiny brook. On a narrow footbridge spanning the brook was a young man and a girl, oblivious to all the world except each other. They stood close together, leaning over the rustic rail, looking down into the water. One of her hands was being clasped tightly by both his.

Dora Jeanne seated herself on a rock in the shade of a willow at the water's edge. Her slippers were filled with sand, a briar had snagged her dress in several places. Her cheeks were hot, her throat parched with thirst. An arrow-shaped sign above her head announced soft drinks. The lane perhaps led to a secluded summer resort farther up the lake shore. She was so thirsty. But it was cool here. And she was where no one could see her. She looked with disapproval at her shimmering striped dress, not at all practical for a day like today; but she had worn it for Jim's sake . . .

The young couple on the bridge — how content they were; her brown hair and his lighter brown, melted together for a moment as he shyly pressed his head against hers, then drew away . . .

O Jim! Jim! I loved you — *I love you now!* But I don't *like* you! I don't like your egotism, your *cynicism,* your rebellion against Christ — *and I don't like mine either!* But —

But Jim is my lover! He wants me. He wants me to marry him and fly away with him. To old Mexico, to the Grand Canyon, to a romantic Guest Ranch in the desert. But I won't *I won't!* I Won't! . . .

The boy and the girl on the rustic old foot-bridge had moved across and were looking down now into the water on this side. Their words were clearly distinguishable to Dora Jeanne's ears, and for the first time she noticed they were sad: "There's no use," he said, "All I hear is war, war, war. I don't expect our country to get into it, but we're bound to get ready for it. Dad says he *knows* there's going to be conscription, and if we'd get married, they'd all say I knew it was coming, and was yellow . . ."

The girl lifted a trembling hand and closed his lips, and in the gesture must have awakened the fire of his love, for he caught her to him and kissed her.

And Dora Jeanne, crouching behind her willow, looked away into the little riffle of the brook that she might not see the beauty and the — pain of it.

And then, without warning, she heard footsteps in the lane above her, and without looking, she knew it was Jim. He had come in search of her.

She knew also that against her better judgment — even against her will — she would let him apologize, and would forgive him; and they would spend the rest of the day together as they had planned — have dinner at an exclusive tea room about which he had told her, and later, they would motor back to Crane Lake and sit on Bailes Martini's wide lawn and watch the fireworks display. He would tell her he was sorry he had acted the fool, that he believed in everything fine and good, and that he loved her.

He would spin again his beautiful web, and she would feel the thrill of being entangled in it, and would not care. She must free Mother from the slavery of debt, send Larry off to the university, change the whole drab Cherryville existence into one of leisure and affluence . . .

She was already clambering up the bank to the lane, where he was waiting.

17

JIM made his apologies, spun again his beautiful web, but things were not the same. At nine they sat in luxurious outdoor furniture on Martini's spacious lawn, watched the fireworks that lit up the sky and the lake in a brilliant and colorful display that was the most gorgeous she had ever seen.

Jim sat beside her, and she let him hold her hand, but the romance of it was gone. She could not yield herself to enjoy a pleasure to which she could not also yield her heart's approval.

Martini — how many years the name had hung over the Lane household like a smothering cloud — "The interest is due next month, and we can't *have* everything we want! Martini expects it in full"; — "No, Dora Jeanne, I'd like to have you in a new dress for the banquet, but the interest, you know"; "I don't know whether we can get the note renewed or not, but we'll try. We've certainly been right on the dot with the interest every time!"

And now, here she was — she, Dora Jeanne, sitting on Martini's lawn in front of his beautiful English-Colonial home — *paid for partly perhaps by money Mother and Larry and Beryl and I have slaved for — and if I want to I can marry Jim and put an end to the whole thing.*

Dora Jeanne watched the glow of Martini's cigar, studied the most unusual face she had ever seen, and wondered at the man. She listened also to their conversation, which was concerning stocks and bonds and John Bishop's lake-front property; and, once when a particularly noisy rocket hissed its way across the sky, and burst into a shower of iridescent eyes that floated slowly down, Martini said, "Fireworks in Europe are getting more violent all the time, and if propaganda over here doesn't stop, we'll be into it, head over heels. As it is now, I expect Washington to put through some sort of compulsory military training bill right away."

Dora Jeanne felt Jim's hand on hers tighten as he said, "And if there's a war, the missionaries and evangelists and college professors and the sick, will be excused from service!" There was bitter sarcasm in his tone.

"And the married. You'll have to be getting on with yours," Martini said, and laughed. He knocked a long ash from his cigar. "Conscription's bound to come. I can *see* it coming. If there's conscription, the government'll set the dead line for marriages along about *now*. They'll have to do that, 'cause the very minute the newspapers start broadcasting the thing, the license bureaus'll be swamped with customers . . ."

Jim's whisper in Dora Jeanne's ear was startling, as he said, "By that time we'll have seen old Mexico and California, and Grand Canyon; and with a little wife on my hands to support we'll be safe —"

She drew away from him, arose suddenly, and with an "Excuse me," went to the white stairway and down to the dock where the runabout was moored, and where she could be alone with her bewildered thoughts. She stood in the shadow of the embankment and looked out across the black lake. The fireworks were over now and except for the little moon there were only the stars to light the sky. Her love had been such a big and beautiful bubble. All evening she had been trying to blow it up again without success. It was only a bubble, and once it had burst, it was gone forever.

Here, at the waters edge, it was so peaceful, with only the soft waves lapping at the dock posts. She seated herself in a deck chair, watched the rise and fall of the runabout in the water. In the past week it had been the white horse on which she and Jim had galloped across the blue desert of the lake; in which she had dreamed and hoped and loved. It had been good fun as well, learning to drive, feeling the thrill that always went with new accomplishment. With Jim sitting facing her in the seat directly in front of the stern, laughing with her, it had been like the beautiful romance of a novel.

But now the bubble was gone. One moment, perfect, iri-descent; the next, a spurt of spray. . . . No more. Always she had been impulsive, — too much so for her own good, some-times. Almost she had decided to marry James Grabill; she would have if his twin had not come at the very moment when she was about to say "yes."

Startlingly now, the thought came to her — a plan full grown. She wished, *how* she wished she was yonder on the black water, with the Speeditwin's throttle wide open, racing into the wind, running away from Martini and Jim and all the past; running away also from a strange future in which there would have been, mingled with all its worldly pleas-ures, only heartache and continued disillusionment. As it had come to her this afternoon under the birches, so now it came again — the desire — the *mad* desire to run away. The boat was here; the motor attached; the electric lantern for night driving needing only to be turned on.

Everything ready? Gasoline, control lever, air vent screw . . .

Far across the lake in the cottage, just up the hill from the Nest, Tim and Beryl and the Spragues were sitting on a wide veranda, watching a quiet moon, and were talking, no doubt, of things in which Jim, up there with Martini, was not inter-ested, but *for which I am so hungry*: THE BEST THING IN LIFE! They would be surprised to see her come roaring up to their dock in the moonlight, but they would be glad to welcome her. Later some of them could drive the runabout home, tow-ing Uncle John's dinghy along behind, for the return trip . . .

Starter rope in place. . . . A sharp pull. . . . A roar of high-powered motor, and she was off, the wind in her face, a thrill of freedom surging within. The best thing in life was not pleasure or success or health or wealth or wisdom or marrying a man who sneered at Christ and His Gospel. The best thing in life was LIFE, and it came to the one who was grafted into the VINE, who gave up one's self in full surrender, not only to receive Him, but to *continually* receive Him. That was what Beryl believed — Beryl and Timothy and the Spragues, — and Mother Lane. . . . Once Mother had had a proposal of marriage from a wealthy man, and because of some firm principle involved, she had not accepted. It was Mother's faith that had carried her through the years. Even Larry had a gruff sort of faith that plunged ahead in the face of difficulties, and trusted Christ to see him through.

For a moment Dora Jeanne looked back at millionaire row, saw the bright lights in the mansions of the wealthy, then she set her face to the black lake, opened the throttle and gave herself to the moments ahead. The moments and the months and the years. She would go back to Cherryville if necessary, and slave along beside Larry and Mother until they raised enough to pay off Martini —

No, *not* Martini! *Jim was the new mortgagee!*

The thought that came to Dora Jeanne now was a cruel thought, but it leaped into her mind fully formed: Jim had taken over the mortgage — he was paying two thousand five hundred dollars *for a wife,* that he might escape the draft, which Martini said was coming soon!

The waves were high now, but she was not afraid. She was only bewildered. It would take a long time for the wound to heal, but she was glad she was running away. The action of the boat now as she shot forward was like that of a galloping horse . . . a white horse . . . galloping, galloping, galloping **on . . .**

18

IT WAS Martini who spoke first, after Dora Jeanne had gone down the white stairway to the dock. He puffed viciously at his cigar for a moment, then growled in an undertone, "How do you manage it, Grabill? Have any difficulty in shifting your affections around like that? I can see how you'd be infatuated with her, but how do you steer yourself away from the last one so quickly? I thought it was Beryl you were going to marry."

"It *was* — I thought so too." Jim cursed and said, "I have a brother. Have had all my harassed life. You know about him. I suppose he'll try to contest the will. You're sure everything's all right?"

"Everything's one hundred percent. The Nest is yours — just as soon as Nature takes the old man. 'Sfunny thing, the way this war spirit affects markets and things. Summer resort business is going to take a fast slide down hill but there'll always be investments and I'm willing to risk what I'm paying you for what I'm getting. I'm practically giving you that Cherryville mortgage, but I'm willing to do that to accommodate you. It's really a neat little fruit farm. All the buildings are in good repair, the fences up, and the soil is fertile."

"Tell me," Jim said, "Do you think I'm safe? Things look pretty bad over there, don't they?"

Martini was deliberate in his reply. "With a wife to support, and no income except what he can earn, a man would have a better chance with a draft board than a single man with no responsibilities; but a single man in good health and the right age is never safe in time of war. You really should have married a long time ago, Grabill."

"I would have, but that fanatical twin of mine stuck his nose into things. I'd have been sitting pretty, with old man Rhinestone's millions waiting to fall into my lap."

"But why cry over spilled millions? It's spilled blood you're worrying about."

And then, from the dock below, came the roar of the Speed-itwin's motor.

Jim started up, but already it was too late. He had only reached the head of the stairway when he saw the runabout shooting at top speed out into the lake. "The little devil!" he muttered, and in his mind's eye he saw again the face of his twin. Timothy Grabill had foiled his plans once more. He knew, without stopping to reason it all out, that he had lost Dora Jeanne. First Bette Lu, then Beryl and now Dora Jeanne — and all on account of Tim and his confounded religion!

Hatred for Tim ran hot in his veins. Martini was right. It was *spilled blood* that was his chief concern. It was Timothy's blood that needed to be spilled — not in war, but by the hand of his own brother! Abel had meddled too long, with his lamb sacrifice, his pious twaddle, his tract distribution. College professor, giving out tracts!

The anger within him was terrific. He knew where she was going, and he would get there first. Tonight there would be a showdown with Tim. He had crossed his plans once too often.

Martini was standing beside him. "Looks like I'm not going to get to finance an airplane honeymoon trip to old Mexico," he said. "Or is she just impulsive? You'll have to corral her, and teach her not to do things like that."

"I'll corral her!" Jim said, over his shoulder. He was already on the run across the lawn toward his car.

Viciously he stepped on the starter, steered out of the drive, drove recklessly through the labyrinth of roads along millionaire row until he reached the highway. On the highway itself it seemed as if there were a thousand cars all racing to get from somewhere to somewhere else. He knew who they were: Families hurrying home from the Aquatennial, young people enroute from one dance pavilion to another — from one roadhouse to another, theater patrons going home. But why did they have to clutter up the road now!

Tim! *Tim! TIM! Professor* Timothy Grabill! All the conflict of the past seemed to rush in upon his mind now: the times when, even as a boy, Tim had beat him in wrestling matches, outrun him in footraces, won higher marks in school — he had chosen the State University purposely that he might not suffer the humiliation of having his brother excel in every class, every athletic contest —!

He would get to the Nest first, be waiting for Dora Jeanne when she came up to the dock. Tim would probably be there also. Tim and Beryl — but that would not matter. He knew what he was going to do.

And while he drove, dodging in and out among the other cars, his anger rose higher and higher until he was taking too many risks. And once, when he narrowly escaped a collision at a cross road, he remembered Martini's words, "A single man in good health and the right age, is never safe" . . . *A man in good health!* The thought was thrown upon the screen of his mind in glaring letters. It hung there, dancing crazily. *A man in good health!* A MAN IN GOOD HEALTH . . .!

———

The four in the cottage had finished washing and drying the dishes, and after a half hour of twilight boating, had beached Uncle John's dinghy on the sands in front of the Nest. Leaving Tim and Beryl to "shift for yourselves awhile," as Geneveve had expressed it, the Spragues had gone up to see that the old man was "safely tucked in" for the night. That too was Geneveve's way of saying it. And she had added, "He's such a precious person, and he's so lonely for his Elizabeth that it seems as if maybe the dear Lord ought to take him home."

On their way to the Nest, Hartford interlocked his arm with that of his wife and said soberly, "He may be taken sooner than any of us think."

"You mean —?"

"Remember I had to run back to the boathouse for more gas before we went boating a while ago?"

"I remember we had to wait."

"The can was empty — completely," Sprague said, "and so also was the motor tank. He had planned to read all afternoon, but he must have changed his mind, and gone out in the boat and —"

Geneveve started, clutched her husband's arm with both hands and exclaimed, "And he ran out of gas and had to row! Dr. Mahone warned him not to!"

Soberly they faced each other, then turned and went up the loggia steps, opened the gate and went inside.

———

Alone now for the first time since mid-afternoon, Beryl and Tim strolled leisurely up the path toward the cottage and the deck chairs which were at the head of the stairs, overlooking the lake and the rocks below.

"Know what I'm thinking about?" Tim asked, when they were comfortably seated facing the lake, listening to the lilting movement of the waves.

"What?" she asked.

"The little minister at the white church. I keep feeling sorry for him that he had to be disappointed. Maybe his wife needed a new hat or something . . ."

"Want to know what *I'm* thinking about?" she asked.

"What?"

"About what a beautiful Bible Conference ground this would make. The Nest for headquarters, with a tabernacle-auditorium out on the point; and beginning here, and dotting the shore all the way up to the promontory where the ducks were playing that afternoon, summer cottages."

It was the first he had thought of it, and he knew the idea was worth giving serious consideration IF the property were his own. He ought to speak to Uncle John about it. His thoughts now, however, were of that afternoon when Jim had gone racing past in the runabout, and a little later had come speeding back with Dora Jeanne.

"Remember the specific name for the wood duck?" he heard himself asking Beryl at this moment.

He could not be sure, of course, but he thought he heard a little sigh escape her lips.

And so they talked, softly and with gentle voices, as lovers approaching the enchanted country. Tim seemed to know that they were at the very gates, and he was surprised at his impatience to enter in, and at the boyish fear that held him back from trying the latch.

And then, suddenly there came from across the lake the drone of a motor at high speed, like an airplane at first, and then distinguishable as an outboard motor. A powerful flashlight swept the beach all the way from the Nest to the cottage, the boat altered its course and steered straight for their dock, while at the same instant, as if timed, automobile head lamps flooded the lawn and the cottage from the opposite direction. For a moment the whole lawn, the beach and the pair on the platform at the head of the stairs, were visible, and then the car lights went out. A door slammed, and footsteps were heard in the path leading to the cottage. *Running* footsteps!

Tim felt his pulse quicken. All afternoon, since the little episode under the birches, when he had seen the fire of intense hate in Jim's eyes, he had known that sooner or later things would come to a climax. Who was driving the boat at such a reckless speed? Jim? or Dora Jeanne? And who was running up the path?

His spirit went suddenly tense. Something tragic was about to happen. He leaped to his feet, caught Beryl by the arm and drew her aside in the shadow of the sumac beside the latticed balustrade of the stairs.

"They've been running a race!" Beryl whispered. "And it looks like a tie! Dora Jeanne's always proposing ridiculous things like that! Sh! ——"

Jim, panting, running hard, flashed out into the moonlight at the head of the stairs, dashed down and reached the dock at the very moment the runabout came gliding in.

A race? Tim would like to believe it. But he could not. He heard Jim's voice, petulant. "Here, give me your hand! Thought you could run away from me, didn't you! Don't you know —?"

And Dora Jeanne's voice, cold, authoritative, "Don't touch me, Jim Grabill!" The watching pair behind the sumac saw them struggle for a moment, saw Dora Jeanne's quick dash for the stairs, and Jim's equally quick dash after her.

"Stop!" Jim's voice demanded. He caught her at the foot of the stairs, swept her in his arms and kissed her while she struck at him helplessly.

"Think I'm going to let you get away from me like that? Not if I know it! That damned twin of mine has tried once too often to run my business!"

Timothy Grabill, lover of beautiful things, was also a hater of brutal and ugly things. They aroused in him — always had — a white wrath which grieved him, made him want to strike and strike until he had dissolved the evil into good. The mystic secret of abiding in the Vine had been his only triumph over his own temper through the years. And he had had a victory that was radiant, because it was not only Christ's victory but the very victory itself WAS *Christ within!*

It was only when circumstances threw him into conflict with Jim that his old nature rose within him, still alive and strong, and refusing to be crucified, demanded the helm of his life, even if for only a moment . . .

And now, in the shadows of the sumac, his hand gripping the warm arm of the girl he loved, hearing himself cursed by his brother, who in life, was like the personification of his own evil nature, knowing that Dora Jeanne was being insulted, he knew that he was going to act.

Even as his body tensed and he leaped to the head of the stairs, he tried to tell himself that he was doing the will of God. He was to be the instrument of God's own wrath against sin.

"JIM GRABILL!" he shouted, and his own voice was like a sword in his heart. O, he hated, *hated* conflict! Hated bitterness, strife, display of temper, evil speaking. These were the activities of the Adam nature within him, not the fruit of the Spirit . . .

The pair, swaying in the moonlight . . . Were they going to fall? There were rocks! . . .

A second later, Dora Jeanne had released herself, and was running up the stairs, where in a moment of emotion she threw herself into Tim's arms.

"Here, Beryl," Timothy said, his voice shaking, *his whole body shaking*, "take her into the cottage. I'll be there in a few minutes." He was gasping for breath . . . O, this is not the Spirit, the lovely dove Spirit. This is *wrath!* This is— this is *hating my brother! O Living Christ, control me!*

He heard the screen door close behind him and knew that the girls had gone inside the porch. And now Jim was coming up, his step heavy, ominous, his shadow on the stairs ahead of him.

Tim waited, his fists clenched, his jaw set. Again came his twin's voice and it was full of curses, low and charged with emotion. "This time," he muttered, "little Abel will not have God on his side! With my bare hands, I'll —!"

Tim remembered the night at the loggia gate, when Jim had derisively called him Abel . . . and *"Abel was such a meddling fool that Cain had to kill him!"* . . . And Timothy knew now, as he had known that night that he could grapple with his adversary-brother and with muscles kept strong by exercise, could hurl his dissipated body to the ground, could lift and carry it to the enbankment and hurtle him down upon the rocks—*where he deserves to be!* WHERE HE DESERVES! No. NO! . . .

He would *not* strike the first blow. He would wait —!

But the first blow was already struck! It crashed against his jaw with terrific impact, jerked his head back. Stars and lightnings shot through his mind and he fell with a thud upon the platform.

Even as he fell, Tim's instinct of self preservation caused his arms to shoot out to protect himself from going over the edge and down to the rocks. They clasped instead of the railing, the knees of his brother, and there were two that fell.

Beryl and Dora Jeanne, standing inside the screen door, clung to each other like rescued passengers from a storm-wrecked ship. They saw — Beryl saw, while Dora Jeanne hid her face against her shoulder — the strange battle in the moonlight — heard the crash as their bodies struck the floor of the wooden platform, heard Jim's curses, their grunts, heard the rip and tear of their clothes, the scrape of their shoes — on the platform at first, and then in the gravel at the edge of the embankment. They were too close to the edge now. *Too terribly close!* Her thoughts were screaming in her mind! Don't! DON'T! Don't let him hurt you, Tim! . . .

The horror of the thing — the sin of it! Brother against brother! She ought to do something! *Must* —!

But she could not move. She was paralyzed. Dora Jeanne was clinging to her like a drowning person, and sobbing and — She could not stand to see it. She turned away, tugged futilely at Dora Jeanne to drag her to the cottage door — and then Dora Jeanne screamed, — a wild blood curdling scream that was like a death scream from another world. And Beryl looked and saw, not two men struggling, but one, standing with hands on hips, and looking down toward the rocks below. His chest was heaving, and he was sobbing in great convulsive sobs. *Only one! Which* one?

Beryl tore herself loose from Dora Jeanne, thrust open the screen door and stumbled across the lawn to the man who stood alone there.

Which one! WHICH ONE! If it were Tim down there on the rocks, —! She reached the head of the stairs. In the moonlight, she could not tell. Which one — *are* you?" she cried to the gasping man in front of her.

And the man laughed a wild triumphant laugh. "I am Cain!" he said. She saw him reach up with his hands and with a gesture that was like that of a mad man, claw his fingers into his hair, while his chest rose and fell violently.

And then she knew which one he was. "You — you've *killed* him!" she cried, and looking down saw her lover sprawled on the rocks at the water's edge. Her lover! My *precious* Tim! She felt the strength of a young tigress pounding in her veins. And in a moment of rage she could have struck out with her bare hands against the face of the man who stood in the moonlight beside her. In a moment of rage, she did strike him. With both hands, on either side of his face. And then, sobbing, she turned and ran down the stairs to her lover.

19

JIM GRABILL stood for a moment, stunned by the swift-ness of her attack. *So!* he thought, the little angel can be vicious! *Both* the Lanes! The one down on the rocks with Tim, and the other who had run away from him. Where was Dora Jeanne now?

From the Nest, running, came again the sound of footsteps. A woman's voice called: "Tim! Where are you? Uncle John is having a sinking spell! He wants you — Where's Tim? Are you —?" It was Geneveve.

"He's at the foot of the stairs," Jim said. "I think maybe he's hurt. Beryl's down there." How coolly he had said it! Beryl's fierce assault on his face had cleared his mind, he thought.

Uncle John, wanting to see *Tim!* What he would have to say would be important.

Geneveve was on the stairs, "Hartford's gone for Dr. Ma-hone!" she called over her shoulder, and disappeared. "Tim! O Tim —!"

James Grabill was already running toward the Nest.

Across the lawn, up the path, past the rose shaded pergola, the bird bath. He reached the loggia gate, swung himself through, thrust open the oak door. There was no light in the great living room except that of the fire in the stone fireplace, which was low. There was a light in the old man's chamber just off the bath. In another instant Jim was there — rather, he was in the doorway. A strange fear gripped him. *This* was death! He had seen death only once, and it had been a death of terror. A classmate had died cursing.

A blue bed lamp shone upon the old man's wrinkled face. He was breathing heavily. Perspiration stood out on his fore-head. His face was already like that of a cadaver . . .

"Tim — othy! Is that — you?" The old eyes did not open. But a hand gestured weakly. "Come closer!

"Kneel, Tim. Beside my bed. I want to b-less you."

He could not refuse. He was still breathing heavily from the struggle, and from the run.

He knelt, with his face against the coverlet of the bed. He lifted the gnarled old hand, placed it upon his head, which was *wet with sweat* — and with blood where Beryl's nails had scratched his face!

The old voice was speaking now — *Hurry, Jim thought, before Tim comes! Say something important!*
". . . bless him and his Beryl. Draw them close to Thyself. Make them happy . . ."

Jim felt the hand on his head tremble; the fingers twitched convulsively. This — *this* was *death!* He couldn't stand it. He had to get away.

Again the cracked old voice, mumbling feebly between breaths, "It's beautiful where I'm going, more beautiful than the Nest, and there'll be a lake, and Elizabeth . . . Be good to Jim, Timothy, you and Beryl. Tell him that I loved him. Beryl helped me write a codicil to my will in which I bequeathed the Nest to you, and five thousand dollars to her to help her in her writing career —"

The old man stopped. He was sighing wearily with every breath, gasping as if he were inhaling death itself . . . "A NEW WILL!" Jim thought. "Bequeathing the Nest to *Tim!*"

Again the old man spoke, — "I'd planned to make a change, to write another one —" Again the old man stopped. There were footsteps scraping on the cement floor of the loggia — the doctor perhaps, with Sprague! Jim pushed aside the old man's hand, looked about for a way to escape, saw on the table beside the bed, the carton of capsules. The lid was off, he noticed, and the carton empty. A sickening sensation rushed in to dominate his mind. What if the old man *were* dying —.

There was no way of escape except the stairway leading up to the sun room. He moved swiftly, silently, and in a fleeting interval was on his way up.

In the sun room, Timothy's study and bed room, Jim looked nervously about. The blinds on the side next to the lake were up, and he could see the cottage and the white platform on which a few minutes ago he and his brother had fought.

There were dark forms on the platform now, but the moonlight was too dim to distinguish who they were. Was it —? Someone was being carried. It was Tim, of course. He had been seriously hurt. *Seriously!* He might be dying — might be — *dead!* It seemed to him a more horrible thing than if Uncle John should also die.

A lifetime of dislike had climaxed in hatred; and hatred, nourished in his mind, had borne the fruit of murder! . . . *And Cain talked with Abel, his brother: and it came to pass when they were in the field, that Cain rose up against Abel, his brother, and slew him.*

The story of the world's first murder had been re-enacted in his mind. Always in his thinking, he had sympathized with the elder brother. Why had not God accepted his offering? And why should Abel's lamb have been preferable?

Standing now, beside his brother's desk, trembling at the thing he had done, bewildered at the things he had heard a moment ago from the old man's lips—: *A new codicil, giving the Nest to Timothy — giving fifty thousand dollars worth of lake front property to Timothy!* — he watched the moving shadows on the platform yonder.

From downstairs, Jim heard Sprague's voice asking, "Are we too late?"

And Dr. Mahone's answer, "Perhaps not. I'll try —"

Suddenly coming down the footpath he saw a woman running. For a moment, she was hidden behind the row of birches. Then she shot out into the moonlight. It was Beryl. Past the rose-shaded pergola, the urn-shaped bird bath, across the wide lawn to the loggia gate . . .

And then her voice, filled with anguish, as she cried, "Quick, Mr. Sprague — Dr. Mahone! Tim's been hurt! He's bleeding —!"

How badly! *"The voice of thy brother's blood crieth to me from the ground!"* God had said to Cain.

From below, Beryl's voice again, "Where's Jim?"

And Jim, crouching behind Timothy's bureau, heard also, a question of fire, demanding, *"Where is Abel, thy brother?"*

Suddenly the sunroom was like a prison . . . Downstairs there was excited talking, footsteps, opening and closing of doors, footsteps on the cement of the loggia, and a man and a woman running across the lawn and up the hill toward the cottage. In only another moment they would bring Tim into the Nest, and —.

Jim tried one of the windows. It opened readily. He lifted his foot, kicked out the screen, pushed his way through and out onto the flat roof. He must see Martini immediately. Evidently, thus far, he knew nothing of the new will, or he would not be negotiating for the lake shore property.

He circled the sun room, walked in its shadow to the roof of the loggia. He must hurry to Martini. Over the edge, he swung his legs and dropped to the ground, and there cursed angrily as sharp pain shot through his right ankle. More provoking still was the fact that Dr. Mahone's car was blocking the drive. There was no way to get his own car to the highway. What —!

The runabout, of course! He would motor across as quickly as he could drive around in his car.

He hurried out across the lawn to the beach, followed the water's edge, dodging willows and birch and rocks, working his way to the foot of the stairs below the cottage. Above him now, he could hear voices, and sobbing, and Beryl's voice saying, "He's dying —!"

He was under the stairway now, crouching in the shadow. He must not let them see him. *"Who* is dying?" his conscience cried, and seemed also to answer, "They're *both* dying!" Both

Tim and Uncle John! The thought struck terror to his heart. He crept toward the dock. His foot slipped and he put out his hand to catch himself from falling, and drew it back. His hand was wet — with blood. He saw it in the moonlight.

He was on the dock now. He was in the boat. He found the starter cord, coiled it, gave a sharp pull. The powerful motor responded with a terrific roar, and in another moment he was away, driving across the lake, straight for Martini's pier. He was running away from a scene of horror, two scenes. Away from murder. Away from his conscience, — which he also carried within him.

The voice of thy brother's blood . . .

He shrugged, drew a handkerchief from his pocket, wiped his face. There was red on the white, and he tossed the handkerchief into the lake. His hand on the rubber grip of the steering-handle trembled so. He was trembling all over from head to foot . . .

Suddenly, as if whispered in his ear by one in league with him, he thought: "Why go to Martini first? Better to find the new will and destroy it. Even Martini would be scrupulous enough to consider the codicil valid, if it were produced by Beryl or anyone."

As suddenly as had come the thought, the prow of the runabout swung sharply to the right, and steered straight for the dock at Beryl's own cottage. Jim remembered now that afternoon a week ago when he had first arrived, and Uncle John and Beryl were there alone. In his mind's eye, he saw the whole thing — Beryl and Tim and the old man had been in conspiracy against him.

20

IT WAS during the strange and weird experiences of that night while Tim waked and slept and waked and slept again; while white-uniformed nurses came and went, when interns stood about his bed watching Dr. Mahone give the transfusion, while also, they fed him through the veins of his left arm, while they came again and again all through the night, with the instrument for taking his blood pressure — In it all, Timothy, under the influence also of powerful drugs to ease the pain of broken bones, felt as never before in his life, the presence of Christ, made real by the Spirit . . . In his thoughts also, he seemed to relive the experiences of the past several hours.

In and out, white starched uniforms rustling, low voices talking, the green-shaded lamp beside his bed casting a soft light over the small two-bed ward . . . The other bed was empty, he noticed, when he first noticed it at all. And it was identical with his own. They were twin beds, he thought. And then he remembered why he was here. There had been a strange wrestling match on a white platform at the top of a high stairs. Brother against brother. Blood against blood. He had not wanted to fight. How strange that these two, *brothers!* who in life had not loved each other, should now be wrapped in each other's arms in what seemed to be a death struggle . . .

Soon, one or the other must fall. Soon, one or the other must be hurled down *down DOWN!* upon the jagged rocks below . . . The pain in his jaws caused by the first blow had disappeared, washed away in the flow of anger in his veins . . . No, no! I do not hate my brother! For he that hateth his brother *is a murderer!* O Father, make me love him! . . .

Cain and Abel! Cain was trying now, to kill him . . . Had the Abel of the Bible tried in any way to defend himself? It was right to defend one's self in emergencies. One was not supposed to be a martyr unless it were necessary, lest he be not a martyr but a suicide.

They were on the gravel now beside the sumac, muscles straining, clothes ripping . . . If only he could pinion his brother to the ground as he had been compelled to do so many times in their boyhood days in order to protect himself from serious injury. If only he could stop those flying knuckles from crashing against his face and head! . . . Wrestling, wrestling. Was it right? Would it not be better to surrender? To acknowledge defeat in order to gain, later, the greater victory of winning his brother to Christ?

"Jim! Let's don't act like wild beasts!" he panted. "Let's—"

Jim's reply had hissed seething hot against his cheek, — *"Coward!"* and he had cursed him.

They were on the edge now. Tim felt his body slipping. His head, his shoulders. In another moment, he would fall, but he would not fall alone. There would be two whose bodies would be broken on the jagged rocks. Two who might be killed. Two to be suddenly ushered into eternity: the one saved; the other *lost!* Jim, in his wrath, did not care . . .

But I care! O my God! I don't want even Jim to be lost! I must go the *extra* mile! . . .

There was no more time to think. Only to act. Only *not* to act, rather! If he held on, *two* would fall!

A moment later, he was over the edge . . . in space . . . falling . . .

———

And now he was here in the little white hospital overlooking the lake. And it was night. He was alive again. It was almost like that — being *alive again,* after going on a long journey into darkness. Only he seemed to be lapsing again and again into unconsciousness. Or was it sleep?

There was only one nurse now, and she was sitting beside his bed, like a white angel. He heard himself talking to her, quoting from a promise made long ago, and from a poem by Annie Johnson Flint:

> *"When thou comest to the waters,*
>   *Deep, the waves may be, and cold;*
> *But Jehovah is our refuge,*
>   *And His promise is our hold . . ."*

He could not remember it all but he knew the way it ended — "Thou shalt not go *down* but *through.*"

"Remember the time, in the New Testament, when there was such a terrific storm on Lake Galilee, and Jesus was asleep in the stern of the little ship? Remember how afraid the disciples were when their ship was filled with water?"

The white angel beside him nodded slowly. "I remember."

"They shouldn't have been afraid." He was speaking slowly, his thoughts threading their way through a maze of strange emotions — "They should have remembered what the Master had said just before they entered the ship. He said: 'Let us pass over to the other side!' If they'd remembered the word US, and believed it . . . I know a beautiful poem about that — *Let US* pass over . . . I'm going to get across all right, don't you think? With *Him* . . ."

For the first time he was aware of the nurse's hand resting on his, steadying him, steadying his rocking little ship. It seemed all right for the nurse, whoever she was — Who *was* she? — to hold his hand. He had wanted to hold her hand last night when they had sat on the stair platform . . . Too bad the little minister had had to be disappointed . . . Stolen data . . . *stolen love* . . .

There were voices in the hall outside, a sound of turning wheels. An ambulance cart swung in at the door, and a voice said, "We'll have to put him here temporarily."

And then another voice, deep and apologetic, "I guess I don't know my own strength, Doctor." It sounded like Sam Grady's voice.

A groan escaped the lips of the new patient as they eased him from the ambulance cart to the bed. The voice, even in a groan, seemed familiar to Tim, but he could not remember where he had heard it — and it didn't seem to matter.

There were nurses, an intern, orderlies. The nurse who had been sitting beside him, was standing now. She was moving away, over to the other bed. She would have two patients to care for now, of course . . . She was going away to tell the disciples, and Peter, that *He Is Risen* —

And then, for a moment, his thoughts carried him away while there was revealed to him a beautiful mystery . . .: The Lord Jesus Christ, for a time, had been imprisoned in His Alabaster Box, but at the cross, he had been released. He, the God of the Universe, had been bruised for our iniquities. He, the Corn of Wheat, had fallen into the ground and died. And after His death, after His *release,* had come the resurrection followed by his many appearances in the New body; there had followed also the ascension into heaven when the gates and the everlasting doors had been opened and lifted up, and He, the King of Glory, had gone in; and after that, — ten days only, — the Holy Spirit had been given to Him by the Father, and He had poured Him forth like fire into every believer's heart — and through them He was now being manifested to all the world . . .

If there had been no cross, there could have been no redemption, no resurrection, no appearances, no ascension, no sent Holy Spirit to annihilate distance and bring Him near and *into* every true believer's body, to indwell . . . to seal . . . to infill . . . to reign . . . to transform . . .

And, Tim thought now, if I had not yielded yonder on the white platform, if I had not allowed my alabaster box to be broken I could not have diffused His fragrance . . . And now I *can* have fellowship with His sufferings . . ."

Incoherently, yet with a beauty and ecstasy beyond anything he had known, the Scriptures unfolded their secret meanings to him. It was not his *physical* suffering that would diffuse the fragrance of Christ, but the crucifying of his self-life, his *selfish* life. In relaxing his hold upon Jim in that death struggle, doing it in order to *save* Jim, he had broken an alabaster box in which his love had been encased — imprisoned, as the Son of God must have felt imprisoned within the body of His humiliation, in which He had been made in the likeness of sinful men . . . But the Cross had released Him. The Cross, the mystery of God. The wisdom of God. The Power of God released —.

————

The girl in white, with blue buttons all the way down the front of her dress to distinguish her from the nurses in the hospital, listened to the nervous breathing of the man who lay in the cot before her. He was sleeping again, as was also the other man in the twin bed across the room. There were only ten feet of space separating these two, but oh, what a great gulf separated them spritually . . .

A nurse came in, and Beryl went out and into the waiting room where Sam Grady and his Molly were sitting, talking with Dora Jeanne and Hartford and Geneveve.

"Strange things are going on in the world tonight," Sam said.

Beryl looked from Sam to Molly to Dora Jeanne to the Spragues. Sam's sonorous voice sounded hollow as he tried to keep it low. He displayed to Beryl the keys to her cottage and to her files. "I don't know what Jim wanted there," he said, "but he got plenty. I was making my round of the cabins when I saw a flashlight playing in your north room. A man was opening and closing drawers, and trying to pry open your files. At first, I thought I'd killed him, when I saw I'd completely knocked him out, but he'll be all right. I twisted his arm a little, I guess. I'm afraid he won't make a very good soldier, in case Uncle Sam needs him in the army we're bound to start building before long . . ."

————

It was past midnight, in the ward where were the twin's beds. Only the dim green light on the table made objects visible. Jim Grabill, awake after having slept, awakened and

slept again, saw the pale face of his brother in the cot opposite, saw a girl, — a nurse, he thought, — in white, sitting beside him. The last thing he remembered, was when he had
been about to close a drawer in Beryl's cabin, and then something hard as steel had struck him on the forehead, and he had
gone out into a strange darkness . . . For a moment, now, as
he looked, he remembered also the battle on the platform,
the nightmare experience at Uncle John's bedside, the flight
into the sun room, the wild terror that had clutched at his
heart, the thrusting open of the screened window of the sun
room and his exit onto the roof of the Nest, the discovery that
his car was blocked in by Dr. Mahone's car in the drive, his
own wild race across the expanse of moonlit lawn, his fear as
he crept forward in the shadow of the birches to the rocks,
his moment of terror under the platform when he had heard
Beryl, sobbing, say, *"He's dying —"* . . . He remembered now
poignantly, the sickening sensation of seeing blood on his bare
hand, when it had touched the rock where Tim had fallen,
and he had remembered the verse: *"Thy brother's blood
crieth to me from the ground!"* — All this, whirling through
his mind now, motored with the accusation of his conscience
that he was indeed his brother's murderer, was driving him into frenzy . . . This was *death!* The girl there, in white, scarcely visible in the diffused light of the green lamp, the cadaver-
ous face of Timothy, — *these* were grim voices crying, "This
is death! *You* are dead!"

Yet, it could not be, because he could hear breathing, could
hear his own breathing, and there was a throbbing pain in
his head — in his forehead. Unless — unless he himself was
Cain, and God had put a mark in his forehead!

He felt himself stirring restlessly, mumbling incoherent
words, and saw the girl in white stand, move toward him, lean
close and look into his face and then turn and move swiftly,
silently, out of the room.

After that, the night dragged on, with nurses and doctors
coming and going — to his bed — to the bed of his brother —

until some time in the early hours of the morning, the ambulance cart came again, silent hands lifted him and wheeled him away . . .

It was not until morning that he knew his brother was alive, and that they had taken him away because Tim must have more quiet, and he couldn't have had that because he, Jim, had been delirious, and because his brother's very life was hanging in the balance.

21.

I T WAS old John Sylvester Bishop who had been dying that night, and it was of him Beryl had spoken when her voice had been heard by the terrified man crouching under the stairs.

And now, the funeral was over. Neither nephew had been able to attend, but both were, to-day, one week later, well on the road to recovery.

Timothy's broken ribs, still heavily taped, were healing satisfactorily, Dr. Mahone had announced after taking an X-ray; and the gash in the back of his head, from which he had bled so profusely, necessitating a transfusion, was now almost entirely healed.

High up on his brother's forehead, to-day, was visible a little red scar, neatly healed. Jim walked with a cane, for it seemed his ankle had been sprained in the struggle with Gorilla Grady, or else when he had leaped from the loggia roof to the ground.

Home from the hospital, and having been ordered by Dr. Mahone to do a little sun bathing, Tim sat now in a reclining position in an orange and green, canopied lawn chair. Beside him was the lady of his heart, with her own chair at an angle so as to face him, reclining lazily, her feet sheathed in blue and white oxfords, herself in the multicolored jumper dress he had liked so well that first afternoon when they had explored the island.

They were looking out now across the lawn to the dock, where her own white boat was beached beside the dinghy. The gulls were busy in their never ending tossings, their mournful voices squeaking even on such a radiant day as this.

It was nine in the morning now. At two this afternoon, Martini would be coming to read the will. What that will might reveal, Beryl did not know. She wondered if the dear old man had remembered to make the new will, as he had told her he would. His lawyer, she had discovered, was Bailes Martini himself. She wondered when the original will had been made, for she knew Martini's files from *a* to *z* and there was no will — there had been no will — there, or any record of any having been made by John Sylvester Bishop.

They had been saying little, these two in their lawn chairs. Contentment, as they had discovered before, did not require conversation.

"How did the writing go this morning?" Tim asked now, his eyes watching a humming bird playing about the roses on the pergola behind Beryl. It was a beautiful little thing, the humming bird, ruby throated, its whole self iridescent, — like the Sponsa Wood Duck — its wings visible in the way an airplane propeller is visible, almost *in*visible. It was not the best time of day for it to be gathering nectar. Evening was better. There had been several of them at the pergola yesterday between six-thirty and seven-thirty . . .

"The writing?" Beryl answered. "Not so well, this morning. I miss Dora Jeanne, — as much as I didn't want her to come, and as much as her gay chatter interrupted my thinking."

Dora Jeanne was already in Cherryville, and had written of her safe arrival, the letter having reached Beryl yesterday. Among other things, the letter said, "Thanks, Beryl, for a whirlwind romance. I'm still all in a whirl, and it's crushing me to be so terribly disillusioned, but I suppose every girl ought to have a similar experience, so she will be on her guard next time . . .

"Listen, Beryl, famous-novelist-to-be, I know I ought not to be saying things about people who are going to be close relatives of yours — and mine — but do you remember the time the lightning killed our horses under the big Sugar tree in our pasture? Well, I don't hold it against our Dear Lord any more, for letting the white horse die, too. Remember what his name was? . . .

"And listen to something else, Beryl —" It was this part of the letter which Beryl was reading to Timothy at this very

moment. She read so enthusiastically, Tim thought, as he
watched the movement of her lips. He was going to like to
have her read to him through the years ahead. They could
come out of their other worlds into a common one by reading
to each other. A gay little sister-in-law like Dora Jeanne would
help him to keep his feet on the earth — "Thanks to you and
Timothy, I have learned to know Christ as my indwelling
Saviour. I don't know exactly when it happened; that is, I
don't know the moment, but it seemed to me, all of a sudden,
while I was on the train, that He drew near, very very near,
and that I just reached up and unlocked the front door of my
stubborn and proud little heart and let Him in. I can't understand it at all, but I'm a new Dora Jeanne. It's like opening a
door, and yet it isn't. It's more like being grafted into the Vine,
and being united to Him vitally, like your Timothy says.
Again it seems as if He just deposited within me a New Life,
and made of me a new center of activity for Himself, with me
being sort of like a new post office in a mighty postal system
of which He is not only the central office, but the whole thing.
Whatever words may be used to explain it, and whatever it
is, it's *Grand!* It's awesome, too.

"I've been devouring Romans eight and those other pas-
sages you told me to read — : Galatians 2:20, 2 Corinthians
5:17, Ephesians 5:18 and that most wonderful passage in John
14, verses 15 to the end of the chapter. It was dear old Uncle
John Bishop who called that to my attention first, one day
when he and I were plowing along in his dinghy. 'Have you
noticed verse twenty-seven, of John 14?' he asked me that day,
and then he said, 'It was when Jesus was on his way to Gethsemane that he gave his peace to his disciples.' He'd read it
that morning in a book, by Max Reich, I think."

There was more, enough to thrill a college professor's heart.
All the philosophy in the world couldn't have done a thing
like that to a person. It was the word of God itself, operated
upon by the Spirit Himself, that had regenerated Dora Jeanne.
The rest of the letter was for Beryl alone. It ran: "So,
Beryl Dear, while the Lane family is passing through its eco-

nomical gethsemane, — seems like sacrilege almost to use the
word like that — we ought to have His peace within us. Anyway, I'm a different Dora Jeanne. And what a different home
we have! I guess the only thing wrong with it was me. Even
my hands are different now. They aren't as fairy-like-dainty as
they were, and it isn't because Mother saves the dish water
for me either! Listen, Beryl-girl, isn't Mother *grand?* I guess
I'm just beginning to get acquainted with her.

"And I guess you're not so *un*-grand yourself. Writing a
book seemed like an easy thing until I saw you actually writing one. I still don't see how you get up so early in the morning, and how you make yourself stay at the typewriter, and
stay and stay and stay and stay, when the lake and the beach
and the whole world of nature are teasing you to come and
play . . .

"I did have a happy time, and a hectic one — and a profitable
one. I suppose my white-horse lover was only making a big
splash when he talked about taking over the mortgage, just
like he was when he painted other soap bubbles for me. At
any rate, Mother hasn't heard anything about it, and Larry
and I are working like Old Dutch Cleanser Twins to help
you and Mother scrape together all we can to pay on the principle when it comes due . . ."

Beryl stopped reading, tucked the letter into its envelope,
for at that moment Jim Grabill came limping down the path
from the cottage, using his cane carefully, yet swinging it in
a manner that would always be characteristic of him. There
was however a certain tenseness on his face as he came toward
them.

At two this afternoon, the truth would be known. The Nest
with its beauty, its grandeur, the flowers, the one hundred
acres of lake front property would belong to — whom? Had
Uncle John made the new will, as he had promised, or had he
forgotten?

Jim stopped directly in front of them, handsome in immaculate white flannels. He was hatless, and except for the tiny
red scar in his forehead, and a peculiar sadness in his eyes, he

and Tim looked exactly alike, Beryl thought. She pitied him that he should have yielded his life to the wrong master.

"A little confession," Jim said, his eyes focused on his brother.

Without waiting for an answer, he went on: "When Uncle John was dying that night and was calling for you, I hurried to his bedside to get his last words. I think maybe I ought to tell you what he said, because I know he thought I was you . . ."

Jim winced as he shifted his position, and a twinge of pain shot through his ankle. "This," he said, and Beryl thought there was a tremor in his voice, — "this was Uncle John's good-by message to you — *'It's beautiful where I am going, more beautiful than the Nest, and there'll be a lake, and Elizabeth . . .'* And then he said there was a codicil in his will, which he had had Beryl write for him, and in that codicil he had left the Nest to you, rather than to me."

Beryl's eyes were studying Jim's. What else had Uncle John said? Had he mentioned the money that was to have been left to her?

She read the truth in Jim's eyes, but he looked away, and said nothing. He was watching the iridescent humming bird flitting from rose to rose.

He turned suddenly to them, drew out his bill-fold, and from it took a folded bit of weather-soiled paper.

"And this," he said, with his jaw set, and the words coming slowly, *"is* the codicil. I found it yonder under the dock beside the dinghy yesterday. I'm sorry there's a hole through it, but I did that with my cane when I picked it up. I thought it was a bit of refuse for the incinerator."

And then, with a puzzling smile upon his lips, Jim Grabill bowed low, handed the weathered scrap of paper to Beryl, turned and limped across the lawn toward the loggia gate.

Timothy remembered then, the night of the storm, when, after hearing the radio's announcement of it, he had gone down to the beach to look after the dinghy. The fairy-like bit of linen he had put into his pocket, to some day return to its owner; the folded piece of what appeared to be scrap paper, he had crumpled in his hand, and tossed toward the lake.

It was a tense moment for Beryl. Except for Jim's explanation, saying old John himself had asked Beryl to write it for him, it would be embarrassing for her to let Tim see the codicil written in her own hand, very confusing indeed to explain why she had not told him before, especially that she herself should have been given such a large amount of money.

Jim's words of a moment ago meant also one other thing: No *new* codicil had been written. On this piece of soiled paper, punctured with the end of a cane, depended very *very* much: her writing career — partly at least, — the paying off of the Cherryville mortgage . . .

Beryl's thoughts knotted themselves suddenly into a bewildered tangle. Dora Jeanne had said that *Jim* had said that Martini had assigned the mortgage over to him . . . Was it true? she wondered . . .

Beautiful little ruby-throated humming bird! How free he was to flit from sweet to sweet, without strain, without anxiety! Clothed in such lustrous splendor. . . . Solomon in all his glory was not arrayed like one of these . . . Consider the fowls of the air, yet "your Heavenly Father feedeth them," the Son of God had said one day. Would not He also care for His own children?

And why had Jim handed it to her at all? Why, when it meant many, many thousands of dollars less for him? For the city property, which the original will was bequeathing to Timothy, was worth so little in comparison to the Nest and the lakeshore estate.

Timothy, in his canopied lawn chair, watched the face of the girl beside him. She was so near that he could have reached out and taken her hand as she had taken his that night in the hospital ward. Nothing seemed to matter to him now, except the WILL of God. His alabaster box had been broken. Here again, was an opportunity to display the love of Christ to his brother.

Uncle John, in the Glory now, possessed of perfect under-standing, — if he could do things over again, would make a will in which his estate would be *equally* divided between the two brothers.

Tim saw the color come and go in the sweet face of the humble Christian girl in whose hands the codicil was clasped. IF that were introduced this afternoon, as an authentic codicil, he would lose all the advantage he had gained. It would steel Jim's heart against him and against the gospel. This moment was his testing time, greater even than that tumultuous moment last week on the platform when he had relaxed every straining muscle in order to save Jim's life.

The city property was enough for him. Let Jim have the Nest. Let nothing *nothing* stand between brother and brother . . .

Suddenly, after he had thought it through, Timothy ex-tended his hand to Beryl for the codicil. There were matches in his pocket which he had put there to be used later in the afternoon, when he and Beryl would go again to their island, make coffee on the little camp stove, sit quietly on the beach until the sun had set, and then motor back in the afterglow . . .

Meticulously, yet as if absent-mindedly, he struck a match, touched it to the paper. A tiny curl of flame shot upward, spread quickly. It finished burning on the grass between them. No movement was made by either of them, no word was said, until only a crinkled bit of black remained.

22

HAVING handed the weather stained old codicil to Beryl,
Jim moved slowly toward the loggia, pushed open the
latticed gate, and went into the Nest. Geneveve Sprague was
arranging flowers on the old oak table in the dining alcove.
Evidently she had not heard him coming for she was humming
a little melody, the words of which were barely distinguishable, yet he caught one significant phrase:

"He is the Source of my contentment . . ."

He limped across the room to Uncle John's favorite chair
by the radio. One burning sentence from old John's dying
confession flashed into his mind . . . *"Tell Jim I loved him . . ."*

He loved me! Me, *ME,* his murderer!

Well, it didn't matter now. There was no such thing as love.
No such thing as faith. Neither was there a God!

And yet if there were no God, then *why should I suffer so
because of my sin?* But there *is* no sin!

Pain, *pain!* The weight of it in his breast was maddening.
It was driving him insane. It was driving the whole world insane. On the world's horizon, *in the world's heart was war,
terrible horrible war!* And if I live, he thought, I shall either
die in battle, or I shall kill someone else. *Someone else besides my Uncle!*

Absently, he picked up from the radio table the very book
the old man had been reading the night before his death.
There was a book mark, and an underscored paragraph. The
words of it seemed to Jim now like mockery, as he read them:

"To the truly repentant soul, who sees by faith the Christ
of the cross as having suffered in his stead, God erases from
HIS memory all his past sins. He dates that man's history
back to Calvary, considers him as having died in His beloved

Son, and gives Him resurrection life *in His Son*. Before a man becomes a Christian, that is, before he has Christ, the Source of LIFE, he has existence only, not Life that is true LIFE. After that, He has LIFE ETERNAL. The Father deposits within that repentant, believing sinner, a *divine nature*. He becomes corporately united, through the instrumentality of the Holy Spirit, to the Source of life and peace and forgiveness and contentment — to God Himself . . . The man passes out of a state of spiritual death into LIFE . . ." John 5:24.

Jim Grabill closed the book. They were burning words. They cut deep. They could, if he would let them, burn out of him the erosion of his conscience; burn into him their fullest meaning.

He let the book fall from his fingers onto the chair, moved now with more determined step toward the stairway and went up — the same stairs up which he had fled the night when Uncle John was dying.

This room, he thought, when he reached the top, is my brother's room. Near the double front window was the writing desk; beside the typewriter, was a manuscript. There was a four-drawer cabinet file to the left. On the desk beside the typewriter, stood a desk pen. There was also a pad of paper.

For a moment, he looked out across the lawn to the rolling lake, saw the flash of gull's wings, heard through the open windows, the rhythmic washing of the waves against the sand, and, farther up the shore, hidden from view because of the hill, he knew the waves were pounding against the rocks.

Below him, beside the pergola, beautiful in its dress of sprawling vines, sat a man and a woman, content in each other's presence. In the woman's hand was the codicil which a few moments ago had been handed to her . . . She was a very lovely woman. So also, had been her sister Dora Jeanne. A man could learn to love either one of them, if he tried, if he believed there was such a thing as true love. But there was no love that would last. Neither between man and woman, nor between brother and brother.

"Well, Little Abel, I didn't kill you. But it is not too late to kill Cain himself."

In Jim Grabill's hand now, lay a blue steel automatic. He lifted it, turned it over, inspected it absent-mindedly.

There was no contentment in this world. There was no peace. The whole world was going to pieces. Going to hell! Mad men ruled it.

He turned to the mirror, pushed his face up close, examined the scar on his forehead, the mark of a would-be Cain. The scar itself was no larger than a bullet wound would make . . .

He would see the hiss of fire as it spat from the muzzle of the gun. He would see the light of his eyes go out — *while it was going out!* The whole world was going mad. *Mad! MAD!*

For a moment he saw reflected in the mirror the lake, the lawn, the pergola, the man and woman resting there. He saw the codicil, now in his brother's hand. Saw also, a quick movement, like a man makes when he strikes a match. Saw the flash of yellow flame, the curl of black smoke, saw the tiny fire burning on the grass between the feet of the man and the woman . . .

Trembling! What made him tremble so? Jim Grabill turned, looked out the window to confirm what the mirror had just told him. The only difference was that now he saw only a bit of crinkled black paper, smoldering in the grass.

He stood staring, still trembling, breathing heavily as if he had run — *and won* — in a terrible race!

He did not move from the window until a wandering wind came and caught up the bit of paper ash, and moved it, tumbling, out across the lawn toward the lake.

Slowly, Jim turned, tucked the gun into his pocket, moved to the stairs, went down. At the radio table, he stopped, picked up the book from the chair, clasped it in both hands tightly, moved across the wide room to the heavy oak door of the loggia, circled the Nest on the opposite side, climbed the hill to the cottage, descended the white stairs to the dock. There was a little nook there, underneath the stairs, where he knew he could be alone.

He walked first out to the very edge of the pier. Far out, as far as a man's arm could throw, was a place where the lake was hundreds of feet deep. Slowly, as if being impelled from within, he took the revolver from his pocket. There was a long, violent over-arm movement. He saw the flash of steel in the air, over and over, like a black gull dying and falling, saw the splash of waves.

There was only the book in his hand now, as he turned and went back to the stairs, made his way along the rocks below until he found a secluded spot under a willow. There he sat down, and opened the book and read.

———

Beryl watched through misty eyes, the burning codicil, as it twisted, curled, blackened. How quickly fire could destroy. She looked now to Timothy's face, and saw there something beautiful, almost beatific.

And when the wind had come, and the bit of ash had blown in fitful movements across the lawn, the gray eyes were raised to meet hers.

She let him look long and deep. What was he seeing there? she wondered. What was there for him to see? And how would he interpret what he saw?

She knew what *she* was seeing. It was the only thing in the whole world that was truly lovely — not the luster of his eyes, not the attractive features, not the personality of the man himself — gracious, refined, self-denying. It was, rather, the *beauty of Jesus*.

And suddenly, she wanted to write, and write and write. To build a beautiful word-house for ten thousand reader-tourists to wander through, and in the house, at the entrance, at the exit, and in every chapter-room, there would be a fountain of water springing up unto everlasting life.

Impulsively, almost abruptly, it seemed to him, she arose.

"Must you go?" He sat forward in his chair. She was restive, like the lake, he thought. She was made for the winds, for flowers and trees, and — the afterglow of summer evenings. She was elusive. The winds of her moods could catch her up and carry her away . . .

"My story," she said. "It's beckoning. Look! See it?" She gestured, not with any movement of her daintily curved arm, but with the inflection of her voice.

He saw. "Thank you," he said. He arose and walked beside her to her boat.

After he had seen her off, and her boat was far out, he turned and walked slowly back to his chair beside the pergola.

The ache in his head, which at times during the past week had been intense, was negligible to-day. There was only the discomfort of the wide strips of adhesive tape on his side where his ribs had been broken.

At his chair, he stopped. He decided he wanted to finish reading Uncle John's book, the one which revealed so many of the deeper things of the Christian life. He had left it in the big chair beside the fireplace.

He watched the maneuverings of the humming bird for a moment before going in. "Little friend," he said musingly. "Don't you ever taste anything but sweets?"

Through the loggia gate, into the great living room, which this afternoon would come into the possession of his brother —. Well, it didn't matter. Nothing mattered except the salvation of his brother's soul — and of his life. If Jim could only know of the Mighty One who, as the book said, "annihilates distance, and brings Christ down from heaven and *into* the very life."

The book, however, was not where he had left it. His eyes circled the room. Genevieve had been there this morning, cleaning. He could hear her now, in another room.

"The book?" she asked when he told her what he wanted.

"I saw Jim take it away with him a little while ago. He —" she stopped when she saw the expression on Tim's face.

"Where is Jim now?" he asked.

"I don't know. He was up in your room a while. When he came down, he picked up the book and went out."

"Where's Hartford this morning?"

"He's in the garage up at the cottage. He wants to get the sailboat finished to-day."

"I think I'll walk up and superintend things," Jim said. "I'll go slow. I still feel a little 'woozy' above the eyebrows."

At the door, he stopped, "Have you seen a letter about here anywhere? I've lost one."

She hadn't.

Slowly, he made his way across the lawn to the footpath going up to the cottage. There was much in the book Jim ought to read, if only he would. There was more. There was a letter to Timothy from Bette Lu Rhinestone, and in that letter -- *In that letter!*

"Make him read the letter, too," he said, as he stopped half way up the hill to rest and to catch his breath.

23.

TIM found Sprague busy at a long table in the garage, putting the finishing touches to the mast of the sailboat. Above the work table, arranged as neatly as dishes in a woman's cupboard, was an array of planes, chisels, drills, saws, files, squares, screwdrivers, hammers, pliers.

They talked for awhile of inconsequential things. Then Sprague looked up from his work, in his hands a beautiful new plane, with chased machine sides and corrugated bottom. "How do you like my new set of carpenter's tools?" He gestured toward the display above the work table. Then he went on, "You'd never guess where they came from."

"Where?"

"From a lady who is a total stranger. A Mrs. Schaeffer heard through her pastor that Jenny and I planned to sail for Africa this fall, and that I needed a new set to take along. Have to build a lot of things over there, you know. So one day last week, presto-chango without warning, here they came. How's that for evidence of the Spirit's guidance."

"I thought the doors had been closed. I thought the war had changed things over there," Tim said, shifting to a more comfortable position on the upside down keg on which he was sitting.

"They're going to open again," Sprague said.

"And until then?"

"Until then, I'm taking care of the little Finnish Sunday school. And while I'm doing that, the Lord is still planing away on me, on both Jenny and me, *finishing us,* so we'll be ready to sail whenever He has Africa ready."

"You're a mystery, Sprague."

"I know it. Jenny told me that this morning. Every born again person is that. Remember the story in John three, of

177

Nicodemus who came to Christ one night for a private interview? Jesus told him that everyone who is born of the Spirit is like the wind, which you hear blowing, but can't tell where it comes from or where it goes. Can you explain a Christian? I mean, a genuine one, in whom the Spirit of God has communicated LIFE?"

A little later, when Sprague was drilling a hole through the top of the mast, he said, "Not that you'd be interested, but it was your little novelist who explained it to Jenny. They were talking about Miss Lane's book, and Jenny said, 'What kind of a story is it going to be?: Adventure, Society, Problem, Love, Psychological?' And Beryl said, 'Mystery.' Then she explained it. I guess her book is nearly finished. Anyway, she says she's taking her hero and heroine up the lake to the little white church and having the twinkly-eyed little minister marry them. And do you know what my Jenny said?" Sprague laughed a mysterious little laugh. "Jenny said, 'Why don't you let Hartford do it? And let me be the bridesmaid?' "

———

With that to think about, Tim went back toward the cottage, following the path that led along the edge of the precipice, past the sumac where, more than a week ago, he had fought a double duel — one with his brother and the other with himself.

To recapture a moment that had been precious to him, in spite of the tenseness of it, Tim stepped from the path into the sumac, and remembered the touch of his hand on the warm arm of the girl who now had become to him the center to which all his thoughts seemed to fly. That was a beautiful thing, Sprague had said: Who could explain a genuine Christian? But it was the indwelling Christ who made him a mystery. And until the Knocking One was admitted entrance, man was only a natural creature, born of the flesh alone. That explained his brother Jim, explained his sinfulness, his love of the world's vanities.

And now, sheltered behind the sumac, there came to Timothy Grabill a deep longing for his brother's salvation, even to being willing to lay down his life; he had burned the codicil; he had removed, as far as he knew, every barrier that stood between them. Could he not now pray with assurance?

And so, kneeling on the cool grass in the shelter of the sumac, Tim prayed for his brother aloud, out of the throne room of his heart.

———

There were two who heard the prayer: One was nearer than near; the other less than fifteen feet away, in a grassy nook under the latticed stairway, a book in his hand. A book and a letter.

The letter, addressed to Timothy Grabill, was back in its envelope. Jim turned it over in his hands. Only a moment ago he had read it. The temptation had been too great and he had yielded, and now he sat musing, moved as he had never been in all his life before. Over and over, like a hammer driving in a nail, the thing pounded in his mind — the thing, written to his brother: "If only Jim knew how much I love him, and that the only reason why I cannot marry him, is because he is at enmity with God!

"I am so sorry if he blames you for it all, but it was not you, but Christ. I realize of course that it was you who were the instrument of the Spirit to tell me of Christ . . ."

If only Jim knew how much I love him . . .! If only Jim knew how much. . . HOW MUCH . . . !

There came to Jim now, also, old John's dying words, spoken supposedly to Tim, *"Tell Jim I love him . . ."*

And there was yet ANOTHER, Who was love personified, Who had given Himself upon a wooden cross on the cranial-shaped hillock above the tombs outside the city gates . . .

Jim started, sat erect. There was a voice at the head of the stairs, where in the moonlight they had fought that night. It was the voice of Tim, the voice of Abel, alive again . . .

And suddenly Jim saw, on the jagged edge of a rock below him, an irregular patch of chocolate brown color. It was the dried blood from his brother's veins. . . . And from above came his brother's voice:

"Oh Heavenly Father, slay the enmity. Break down this terrible wall that stands between us — this hedge wall. I am willing, if necessary, to take every thorn, if only he may know Thee . . ."

———

The praying man was being swept along in his prayer by the Spirit, pouring out strong cryings, lost in the sweetness of the presence of his God, yet suffering pain because of the burden, when suddenly he heard a step on the stair, then another and another. Slowly, steadily, assisted by a cane . . .

And from below came also his brother's voice, a strange sobbing voice that was like the tearing open of a heart. "TIM! Wait ——!"

And there, on the white platform they met, these two. In the background was the flaming sumac, the white latticed balustrade; below them the blue lake, with white caps breaking; and across the bay — in her cabin, a young woman was writing the closing chapters of her novel, which when published, would bear the title, stamped in gold, A CUP OF COLD WATER.

Hartford Sprague, emerging from the garage and walking toward the cottage, stopped in the flower-bordered path. Two men were standing on the platform at the head of the stairs, their arms about each other. Both were sobbing and saying things which were not meant for other ears to hear.

Abruptly, his heart pounding, Hartford Sprague turned, circled the cottage, and ran as fast as he could to Geneveve to tell her the news and to take her in his arms with deeper love because of what he had seen.

24.

THE war in Europe had reached new heights, unleashing new fury, screaming to the world the corruption of the human heart. The war. The *war*. The *WAR!* It was one year old this week. Its storm center now was London, England's capital.

Jim Grabill, this September morning, moved slowly from the loggia gate out across the lawn to the beach to where old John's dinghy was waiting. In his hand as he walked — and limped as he walked — was old John's silver-topped cane. In his mind was only restlessness.

Reconciliation with his brother was only a step in the direction he was to continue to go. There was no enmity now against the one whom he had hated so many years, and whom in the fierceness of his anger, he had tried to kill.

Reconciled with his brother, yet there was no peace. For was he not also the murderer of his Uncle John! Oh, they had told him about the gasoline tank being empty, and how the old man had not only had to row home the afternoon preceding that fatal night, but on that day also, the monster wall-eye had struck and the old man had worn himself out, trying to land it. This, Uncle John had confessed to the Spragues that night, before his sinking spell from which he did not rally.

And yet, Jim thought now — had been thinking also, during the past weeks —, would Uncle John have over-exerted his heart if he had been rebuilding his strength by taking the capsules . . . ?

Torment, day and night, had haunted him, until today he had resolved to confess the thing to Tim. Could God forgive murder also? In himself he could see one Judas Iscariot, hating the thirty pieces of silver which he had gained by betraying the Lord Jesus Christ unto death. He saw that despised man hurrying back to the priests, and in despair unspeakable tossing the blood money onto the floor and then rushing away to take his own life. He, Jim, had planned that also, but had been stopped by a Hand. He was driving now across the bay to Beryl, to get rid of some of the money, to do good with that which was born of selfishness.

———

Back again, Tim met him at the dock, and together they walked across the wide lawn toward outdoor chairs beside the pergola.

Seated, Jim lifted the silver-topped cane, studied the gnarled grain of the wood. To their left, at the foot of the path leading up to the cottage and the platform, was Sprague, stopping to make some adjustment on a power lawn-mower. A moment later the motor was chugging away, and Sprague following it forth and back along the farther edge of the great lawn.

Jim cleared his throat, "You're to be congratulated, Tim," he said. "She was made for you. She's a wonderful girl. She's never tasted the world, and she'll never know the bitterness that comes when conscience condemns and keeps on condemning. She finished her book this morning . . .

"Listen, Tim," — He felt the words rushing to his lips. He was going to confess the terrible thing he had done. He could not get the stains off his mind; off his hands; off his soul . . . "Tell me, — Can — Does God forgive — *murder?*" The word was a whisper. He was aware of the loud beating of his heart, the trembling of his nerves, the hatred of himself and all that he had been all these years.

Tim's face did not betray the emotion he felt. He looked now into his brother's eyes, saw the misery in them, saw also the tiny scar which was the mark of Cain in his forehead. Jim was thinking, perhaps, of his intent to kill him, and the Spirit was convicting him of that as being murderous. For "whoso hateth his brother *IS* a murderer."

Quietly, from the Scriptures, Tim quoted while beside them there flitted from rose to rose, an iridescent humming bird.

He could hear the humming of its wings, like — like the humming of airplane motors over a besieged city, — " 'Though your sins be as scarlet, they shall be as white as snow; though they be red like crimson, they shall be as wool.' "

It was like looking into a mirror, to watch Jim's face now, it was so like his own; the eyes were like his own when for some reason there had been heartache . . .

"Remember that night at the loggia gate when we almost fought?" Jim asked.

"I remember."

"That was the night I — Remember I brought the capsules for Uncle John and — and left them on the radio table?"

Jim swallowed hard. This was maddening. Why didn't he burst out with the confession? Why didn't he conquer his cowardice? Why —

"Funny thing about that night," Tim broke into his thoughts. "You know, I'd just been to the doctor myself, right after that, and had brought out a second carton. "I —" And now Timothy felt his own heart pounding. Had Jim talked with Dr. Mahone? Did he know about the second carton? Was he wondering now what had become of it? Did Jim suspect that he had doubted him that night? Ought he to confess that?

It did not seem right or necessary that he should.

Jim was leaning forward now, perspiration standing out like little beads on his forehead. "What," he said, "became of the — I haven't seen it. He used only one carton, didn't he?"

Like a flash Tim saw the way out. He must *not* let his brother know how he had doubted him that night, that he had been afraid . . .

"The second?" He extended his arm toward the pergola, picked a new rose, twisted the stem, watched the rose twirl beautifully, then he said, "Maybe it was wasteful, but — well anyway I threw it into the fire. Ah —" It was not necessary to tell Jim *when* he had burned it. Not at all . . .

"You mean —"Jim leaned forward tensely. "You burned — you mean the one I brought, or yours?"

"The one you left on the table." Tim said the words and looked to see if Jim was startled by them. He saw in those blue eyes below the scar an expression which was strange indeed, and he wondered what emotions stirred there, but he would not ask. Sprague was coming now, following the wake of his mower, cutting a swath beside the stone path that led to the beach.

Jim arose abruptly, mysteriously, Tim thought, and with an "Excuse me," limped toward the Nest.

———

At the loggia gate Jim stopped, looked toward the sky, over the tops of the high pines to where a great cumulous cloud hung, like a wool pack piled tier on tier — like a great white stairway leading up to heaven itself. And from his lips there burst strange new words as he said, "I thank Thee, Father! Oh, I thank Thee!" And as he entered the Nest, he recalled something read in a book, "Justified really means 'just-as-if-I'd.' God looks at me when I am in Christ, *just-as-if-I'd never sinned at all.*" And remembering it, he understood the meaning of the Grace of God. There was nothing against Him any more. Christ had taken the whole blame, blotted it out forever. He pushed open the oak door, entered the living room.

At the radio he stopped. A truth so tremendous, so soul-revolutionizing, was worth a man giving his life for. Soon the government would be asking all young men to give one year of their lives for defense preparation. Now, also, the Governor of the universe was asking for all his life.

He had asked for it, and He should have it. *He has it now.*

25

IT HAD been a climactic day for Beryl, this brilliant early September day. There had been many climactic events, each succeeding one more colorful than the last.

And now the day was to be diademed with a sail on the lake with Tim who at this very moment was on his way across the bay. Beside Beryl now as she stood on her cottage porch waiting, was the little table, the design on whose lamp shade was a miniature gold-trimmed ship, with its blue sail unfurled to the wind. Beside the lamp, neatly typed and boxed, wrapped and ready for mailing, was her book manuscript. Early this morning she had typed the final chapter, read and reread it many times, as she had the entire manuscript.

Tomorrow she would be on the train for Cherryville, in her possession certain valuable papers having to do with the mortgage. James had come this morning bringing the papers which would set the Lanes forever free from its slavery. In addition Beryl would carry a certified check for five thousand dollars, from the Bishop estate, Jim being responsible for that also.

It was a new James Grabill, humble and repentant, who had driven over this morning in Uncle John's ancient dinghy. He had gone away equally humble and, she knew, with a dissatisfied heart and mind. Watching him go, a lonely figure in the stern of the boat where so many hundreds of times old John had sat, Beryl had thought of one Judas Iscariot, who for thirty pieces of silver had betrayed his Lord unto death, and then had not wanted the silver. Always it was like that — painted pleasures inviting the taste; the taste causing pain and heartache and spiritual disappointment. Why was he so sad? she wondered. Had he not all the money he needed? Perhaps he had not entered the light of full assurance of salvation. Perhaps he was still trying to build upon emotions rather than upon the Book.

That had been the climax number one. The second had followed almost immediately. There had been a letter from Mrs. Schaeffer, part of which had said:

"I have finished reading the carbon copy of your story to date, and, dear Beryl, I am convinced our leading was definitely of the Spirit. COLD water, the EXTRA thing, the SACRIFICIAL thing, the COURTEOUS thing, the SECOND-MILE thing, the dying-to-self and the living-unto-Christ philosophy of life is the secret of harmony. It is the oil that minimizes friction. One must have Christ within of course in order to manifest Him to others; and this comes about only by the new birth; but after LIFE has been implanted, it must be nourished and exercised and revealed to others. Self life must be starved out . . .

"Let me quote, Beryl, from an old letter of yours, written on the fourth of July. You misspelled one word, which I am underscoring for emphasis. Unwittingly, you wrote a tremendous truth, I believe. Here is the paragraph:

" 'It seems to me now as I write this, and while the dear Holy Spirit is making the presence of God so real, that I have been *fire*ordained to this work —'

"I know of course, Beryl, that you meant to say *fore*ordained, yet it seems to me the two are inseparable: The foreordained writer or missionary or other Christian worker will be *fire*ordained. The Fire of the Lord Himself will burn within . . ."

The climax of the letter itself was —

"This week I have been doing a little business with your former employer, Bailes Martini, and have purchased the eighty acres of lake shore property directly across the bay from where you are now. No more ideal location could be found for a Bible conference ground for young people. . . . Maybe you'd be interested to know it was 'your Tim' who suggested it to me . . ."

It had been a beautiful letter and filled with encouragement. It lay now beside the manuscript waiting to be shared with Tim when he came.

When he came. Slowly Beryl turned, lifted the manuscript and the letter, pushed open the screen door and went out and down the steps to the board walk. She planned to meet him at the dock. It was going to be their last time together for a long time, and she wished to re-live some of the moments of their first meeting. Tomorrow, also, he must drive back to Phillips to prepare for the fall term of school.

It was a beautiful thing to watch — Tim's sailboat moving like a great white swan across the blue lake, Timothy himself in white, the blue water as blue as the sky itself, the sail like a white cloud drifting. There were many adverse winds in life, but it was "the set of the sail, and not the gale," that determined the way one went.

Behind her, as she waited, came Big Sam Grady, to go down to the dock with her that he might steady the boat, until she was seated.

Amusingly gruff as usual, he said when they were ready to go: "If you cause Molly and I any worry by not coming in before dark, we'll not let you go out together again this year! Understand?"

They were off.

Sprague's sailboat was the utility type, which could be used for rowing, motoring or sailing. Rigged for sailing, Tim and Beryl had used it again and again during the past few weeks.

He seated her directly in front of and facing him, neatly pillowed and low enough so that her goldenrod hair would feel only the passing wind when the boom should swing from fore to aft or vice versa.

Silently, as silent as the white clouds overhead, they glided out across the bay, the boom jibing fore or aft as the caprice of the wind might make necessary.

Their talk was as it had been that night on the platform in front of the Sprague's cottage. They knew they were lovers approaching the enchanted country. They were sailing toward their island now; sailing toward it, and exploring it at the same time.

They could have talked of the war that now was tearing out the heart of Europe, laying waste nation after nation; that was stirring the minds of thinking men the world over. They had talked of it before, and had turned their conversation gladly to other things, to things spiritual and beautiful and holy. They had played, too, during the past weeks, — tennis, fishing, swimming, motor-boating.

One hand on the tiller now, the other guiding the boom, he watched her face. It had become a habit with them, sailing like this on a quiet day, saying little, looking deep into each others eyes — saying so much, so very much, reading all about the enchanted country before they entered it.

Out and out, past the Nest, the cottage dock, along the shore toward the promontory where the wood ducks played . . .

Looking up, they saw Jim standing at the head of the stairs. They waved to him. He lifted a hand in slow salute, dropped it to his side, stood immobile, as if seeing them had turned his thoughts aside, or sent them spinning along on a trail of his own. Then he turned and limped slowly toward the cottage.

They were passing the promontory now. The row of vertabrae-like rocks pushed out almost to where they were. There were no wood ducks today, but Tim knew they were both remembering the afternoon when they had seen them the first time, and when he had given her the object lesson from the linden leaf: the heart-shaped leaf, the little bract attached to the base of the stem, the stem of the flower cluster vitally connected with the central vein of the miniature leaf, the creamy yellow flowers giving off the sweetest of perfume.

It would soon be autumn now — goldenrod time. Classroom time at Phillips, apple picking time at Cherryville. She was going home, but on a week-end he would follow her there.

He would spend his Thanksgiving and Christmas vacation there, meet Dora Jeanne again, and Larry and Mother Lane . .

And in Europe the war would roar on like a storm blowing out of hell, and American men would be called to enlist, to prepare for defense.

War . . . France, Belgium, Holland, Poland, England. . . . What the whole world needed was only Jesus, the *Lord* Jesus Christ. . . . But it would not have Him.

For the first time, then, he saw her book manuscript, wrapped and ready for mailing. His own was also ready, waiting only for the dedication. He had been thinking about that — to whom it should be dedicated. He had a question to ask her concerning it this afternoon. He was going to ask it now, most any time. He would wait though, until a little later, until they were on their way back. This was to be their last time together, except for the brief interval tomorrow when he should drive her to her train.

Yes, Europe needed Only Jesus. He had read something this morning by Norman P. Grubb of London — not about war, but about peace, the peace of the soul that is trusting in Jesus. It was too good to keep. It must be passed on and on and on.

"Remember the song we sing sometimes in our churches: 'I Need Thee Every Hour'?" he asked.

She nodded, "I like it very much."

"The chorus goes: 'I need Thee, oh, I need Thee.' "

She nodded again, listened while he sang it. They had been singing duets on Sundays in the little Finnish church.

"Here's a new version of it I read this morning," he said. "It's the song of the flower cluster, singing to the linden tree, the Source of all its life:

" 'I *have* Thee, oh, I *have* Thee,
Ev'ry hour I *have* Thee . . .' "

It was more than beautiful. It was the Vine again. The Vine and the branches, and the continuous inflowing Life . . .

Around the promontory there was barely enough wind to keep the boat moving. At intervals the boat stopped entirely, and they sat basking in the sun, waiting for a breeze, from this way or that, to carry them on.

It was a favorable time to discuss with her the dedication of his new book. They were far out from shore now, with not a breath of wind. The blue water here seemed as clear as the sky itself, with only occasional foam clusters like clouds floating. He knew there ought to be a moon, and lilacs or honeysuckle, rather than a blazing sun and tossing gulls. The gulls, a half dozen of them, had been following along, complaining, accepting the bits of bread Beryl tossed into the lake for them, and squeaking for more, coming down for each morsel like a bomber doing a power dive . . .

But there was no moon, no lilacs or honeysuckle. Neither were they necessary. "Remember the little minister —" he began.

A gull swooped low, fluttered about her hand as she extended a crust of bread. Her heart warned her of what was coming. She would feign indifference — if she could. Her fingers trembled. The crust of bread dropped into the water. The gull swooped upon it, and was away.

"Sprague told *me* Jenny told *him* you told *her* you took the hero and heroine of your story to the little white church for their wedding. You did that without my consent."

She was watching the gulls, avoiding his eyes; deliberately, he thought. "Was the idea copyrighted?" she asked.

"I thought of it first."

"And whose fault was that?"

"Yours. You stole information from the bulletin board."

They were at the gate now, his hand was on the latch. He was thinking of their first night together at the Sprague's cottage, when she had stolen his "love." *And had not yet returned it!*

And then, without letting himself wait any longer, he was trying the latch. He forgot the necessity of a moon and of flower fragrance. He leaned forward, caught both her hands in his. Their eyes met also, and clung, and he was saying, "Are you ready now to return — what you stole that night? So — I can take *my* heroine to the little minister?"

It was the supreme moment of her life. She felt his warm hands clinging to hers, felt the intensity of the man, the strength of his love, the beauty of it. The power of it was gathering her up into his very self, and making her one with him forever. Her hands caught fire from his and she knew she was going to say, "I am ready . . ."

And then, at this, the greatest moment of her life, a cross wind caught the sail, and swept it in a wide horizontal arc. The boom swung sharply away. Tim grasped the control rope with one hand, the tiller with the other.

It was a full half minute before he had the boat under his will, and they were moving with the wind and the ruffled water out toward the center of the lake.

It was a tremendous moment for them, disappointing, a bit confusing, until they regained their poise.

Then suddenly, she leaned back upon her pillows, relaxed, and laughed, and said, "That *had* to happen before I mailed my book to the publisher. I wasn't quite satisfied with the way the final scene was done. It was a bit too common — he, proposing in the moonlight behind the sumac. I'm going to change it. I'm going to make him do it at midday, under a sweltering sun, while the wind is blowing at a time when, even if she had said 'yes,' he couldn't have taken her in his arms —"

"Even if?" he asked.

She finished the sentence she had begun, saying, "Until later."

"That's a promise," he said and because of the wind, gave his attention to the boat."

"You don't mind if I use it in my story?" she asked.

"Not at all," he said, and swung the boom from fore to aft and set the propeller in the opposite direction. "But you must remember it was my idea. I thought of it first."

"I'm not so sure." It was a confession.

"And it'll have to end exactly the way I want it to. Promise me that?"

"I promise." And with the promise went her heart, and all her future. "Forever and ever and ever," she added. There was nothing new in what she had said but it was new to them and would continue to be new forever and ever and ever.

He had not asked her about the dedication of his book — to whom to dedicate it, but he would not need to ask. He could surprise her by having it read, as he had already planned:

"To My Beloved Wife."

THE END